THE LAST SURPRISE

"Slocum!"

The unexpected use of his name caused Slocum to whirl about and stare Carbuncle right in the eye. It was a toss-up which man was more surprised.

"How'd you—" Carbuncle wasn't the quickest thinker in the world, but he knew Slocum shouldn't be in the Breiland Institute for the Insane. The outlaw went for his pocket and had a derringer half pulled out when Slocum reacted. He bent, grabbed the handle of his knife, and swept up in a smooth motion that ended with the blade buried in Carbuncle's chest. Slocum felt the tip of the blade bounce off a rib and then slice through the man's heart. Carbuncle looked down at the blade in his chest, then up at Slocum.

"No," he said in a curiously ordinary voice, and then he died.

JAKE LOGAN

SLOCUM
AND THE
MADHOUSE MADAM

JOVE BOOKS, NEW YORK

THE BERKLEY PUBLISHING GROUP
Published by the Penguin Group
Penguin Group (USA) Inc.
375 Hudson Street, New York, New York 10014, USA
Penguin Group (Canada), 90 Eglinton Avenue East, Suite 700, Toronto, Ontario M4P 2Y3, Canada
(a division of Pearson Penguin Canada Inc.)
Penguin Books Ltd., 80 Strand, London WC2R 0RL, England
Penguin Group Ireland, 25 St. Stephen's Green, Dublin 2, Ireland (a division of Penguin Books Ltd.)
Penguin Group (Australia), 250 Camberwell Road, Camberwell, Victoria 3124, Australia
(a division of Pearson Australia Group Pty. Ltd.)
Penguin Books India Pvt. Ltd., 11 Community Centre, Panchsheel Park, New Delhi—110 017, India
Penguin Group (NZ), Cnr. Airborne and Rosedale Roads, Albany, Auckland 1310, New Zealand
(a division of Pearson New Zealand Ltd.)
Penguin Books (South Africa) (Pty.) Ltd., 24 Sturdee Avenue, Rosebank, Johannesburg 2196,
South Africa

Penguin Books Ltd., Registered Offices: 80 Strand, London WC2R 0RL, England

This is a work of fiction. Names, characters, places, and incidents either are the product of the author's imagination or are used fictitiously, and any resemblance to actual persons, living or dead, business establishments, events, or locales is entirely coincidental.

SLOCUM AND THE MADHOUSE MADAM

A Jove Book / published by arrangement with the author

PRINTING HISTORY
Jove edition / October 2006

ISBN: 0-515-14207-7

JOVE®
Jove Books are published by The Berkley Publishing Group,
a division of Penguin Group (USA) Inc.,
375 Hudson Street, New York, New York 10014.
JOVE is a registered trademark of Penguin Group (USA) Inc.
The "J" design is a trademark belonging to Penguin Group (USA) Inc.

PRINTED IN THE UNITED STATES OF AMERICA

10 9 8 7 6 5 4 3 2 1

1

John Slocum fought to keep from doing something he would regret. His gun hand twitched, and he longed to grab the Colt Navy slung in his cross-draw holster and lay the barrel alongside this son of a bitch's head.

"You mind repeating that, Mr. Wilson?" Slocum's green eyes bored into the banker's muddy-brown eyes, but the banker did not budge an inch. If anything, Slocum thought a small smile tried to lift the corners of the man's mustaches. He knew he held the upper hand, and Slocum was the loser. That didn't make it any easier to swallow that he was stealing.

"I think I have been plain enough, Mr. Sloan."

"Slocum. The name's Slocum."

"Ah, yes, quite," Wilson said, leaning back in his fancy chair and tenting his fingers. He rested his hands on his thin chest and continued to give Slocum the "gotcha" look.

As he'd entered, Slocum had noticed the bank guards, both with rifles placed behind metal plates on either side of the bank lobby. It would take a small howitzer to stop either of them. There might even be a third guard lurking somewhere in the rear of the bank, possibly near the vault.

Its huge door stood tantalizingly open, as if Wilson wanted to further torment Slocum.

"You have eight hundred dollars of my money," Slocum said coldly. "I won it in a game over at the Longhorn Drinking Emporium two nights ago. I put it into your bank then for safekeeping, and I want it back now."

"The Farmer's and Rancher's Bank of Austin knows nothing of any such deposit."

"I've got the deposit slip here," Slocum said. "The teller wouldn't honor it. That's why he sent me to you. You were the one who took my money."

Wilson glanced at the slip of paper and shook his head.

"I don't know what's going on, Mr. Sloan or Slocum or whatever you said your name is, but that's not my signature. It's not my name nor is it even on an official bank form. I suspect you scribbled it out yourself, if you can write. If you can't, you got someone else in Austin to do it for you."

"I'm not cheating you," Slocum said, anger rising. "I came to the bank, knocked on the door, and you were working late."

"I sometimes do, but never would I open the door when I am alone," Wilson said smugly. "But go on. Tell me the rest of your fairy tale."

"You sat in that very chair, you took my money, you scrawled the receipt and said you'd put the money in the vault."

"A pretty tale, but one with gaping holes. The receipt isn't genuine, that's not my signature—but more than that, why would a man such as yourself want to put anything into my bank for safekeeping?"

"The man I won it from was threatening to get some ranch hands he works with. I didn't want the money on me if I had to deal with them."

"So it would have been all right if they had killed you, but this supposed money wouldn't have gone to them?" Wilson guffawed. "That is rich, sir. I thought I'd heard every possible swindle in my day, but this one takes the cake."

"It's not a swindle on my part. I want my money."

"How dare you accuse me of stealing from you!"

"Reckon I ought to tell the marshal?"

"Go on, tell Jethro. Say howdy to him for me. He's my brother."

"I'll get a lawyer."

"Out of fourteen lawyers, Aaron's the only lawyer in town worth his salt and he's my son." Wilson was looking like the cat that had eaten the canary. "You have to go far and wide to find anyone who'll believe you for even an instant, Slocum."

"At least you got the name right now," Slocum said, standing. He heard rifle hammers drawing back with metallic clicks. From the vault came a stubby man swinging a sawed-off shotgun around like a conductor's baton.

"You want this . . . gentleman escorted out, Mr. Wilson?" asked the shotgun guard.

"If necessary." Wilson looked at Slocum with a smile that made Slocum want to knock out the man's teeth.

"You always have so many hired guns around?" Slocum asked.

"We have had an unusual number of robberies lately. I feel it is prudent to protect my depositors' assets," Wilson said.

"They might protect the money from outlaws," Slocum said, "but who protects your depositors from you?"

"Get him out, McGee," snapped Wilson. "I've had enough of his insinuation and outright insults."

Slocum swung about and walked from the bank, seething. He had never figured a banker to rob him in the way Wilson had. Wilson might foreclose on widows and throw them into the street for not paying mortgages, but Slocum had thought the man would be honest when it came to taking money destined to be stashed in the vault. He had been wrong. He had been wrong to the sorry tune of eight hundred dollars.

Outside, in the middle of the street, Slocum turned and

looked back at the bank. It might as well have been a cavalry outpost since it was so heavily guarded. The look he had gotten at the vault told him it would take a crate of dynamite to blow open the safe door. That much explosive was likely to destroy whatever was inside. Slocum's dark thoughts turned to doing just that. It'd show Wilson.

Destroying the vault wouldn't hurt Wilson one iota, Slocum guessed. Knowing how the banker worked, Slocum didn't doubt Wilson had stashed as much as he could in a valise somewhere outside the bank so he could proclaim all the vault contents destroyed. Then he would get his brother, the town marshal, to come after Slocum and chase him to the ends of the earth.

Still, losing so much money, even if it had been in greenbacks, galled Slocum something fierce.

It was only midday, but Slocum went to the Longhorn for a drink. He still had a few dollars stuffed in his shirt pocket. Enough for a shot of whiskey, but hardly enough to get into another poker game.

With the way his luck was running, he would probably have a straight flush and lose to a royal flush.

There were a few earnest imbibers already working on a drink. Mostly warm beer from the looks of them, though three men at a back table had a bottle of rye they were passing around. Slocum paid them scant attention as he went to the bar. He stared ahead into the well-polished mirror and saw that he looked like he was going to chew nails and spit tacks. He tried to cool down, but it didn't work. The more he thought of Wilson and his thieving ways, the madder he got.

"What'll it be, mister?" the barkeep called from the far end of the polished oak bar. He kept one hand under the bar, probably on a six-shooter if Slocum took offense.

"Whiskey," Slocum said. "Make it the good stuff, not that lizard pizzle you serve out of those bottles." He pointed to a row of half-filled bottles lining the back bar. All bartenders kept a special bottle where the customers couldn't see it and think they were entitled to the same rotgut the rich and powerful drank when they bellied up to the same bar.

"Fifty cents a shot," the man said, "but ya kin afford it. Ya won that pile of money the other night, din't ya?"

"Yeah," Slocum said.

He took the whiskey and sipped it. The price was high, but the whiskey was good. Slocum let it wash over his lips and bathe his tongue before sliding down smooth as silk. When it hit his belly, a warmth spread throughout his body. It took away some of the anger he felt, not much but enough.

"You got the look of a man who can use that hogleg."

Slocum turned to see the tallest of the trio from the back table leaning on the bar a couple feet away. The man had both elbows securely planted to show he wasn't a threat. Slocum didn't know if he read the man right, but there was something cold and calculating about him.

"I prefer to drink alone," Slocum said.

"That's a shame since me and my two friends—that's them back there—wanted to invite you to join us. My treat. Not as good as that tarantula juice, but the price is better."

"You're standing me a drink?" Slocum knew now something was wrong. Strangers didn't come up like this, even if they were friendly Texans.

"Why the hell not? You got such a hangdog look, might be we can cheer you up."

"Why'd you want to do a thing like that?" Slocum knocked back the rest of his whiskey. It puddled in his belly and sent shivers throughout his body.

"Might just be we can help each other. Come on over and set a spell. Listen to what we're proposin' and if you don't like it, have another drink and be on your way."

Slocum silently followed the man to the table.

"These are my amigos. That scruffy-lookin' one's Kinsley and the really scruffy one's Carbuncle. Me, I go by Laramie." He thrust out his hand.

Slocum moved to keep Laramie between him and his two friends as he shook. The grip was firm and welcoming. This made Slocum even warier. He slid into a chair across from Laramie, with the other two on either side.

"You got a look 'bout you, you do," said Carbuncle. "We kin use a man like you."

"Shut up, Carbuncle," said Laramie. "Let the man enjoy a drink 'fore we get down to business."

Slocum looked the trio over good and hard. Carbuncle didn't look too smart, and he shot his mouth off. He wore a tattered black cloth coat and a brocade vest two sizes too large for him. A tarnished gold chain hung from a button and vanished into a watch pocket. Slocum doubted there was a watch attached. Kinsley was hardly better dressed. He looked more like a prospector in his canvas pants and red-and-black-checked shirt. What he lacked in sartorial splendor he made up for with the pistols he had hidden on his body. He wore two six-shooters butt-end-forward at his hips, but Slocum saw a belly gun tucked into a side pocket and figured the bulge in the shirt pocket came from a derringer.

These were two owlhoots if he had ever seen them. And that went double for Laramie. Slocum didn't doubt Laramie had more than one wanted poster dogging his tracks, not that the man would be unique in that. Slocum had more than one chasing him, too.

After he had been shot in the gut by Bloody Bill Anderson for protesting Quantrill's policy of killing all males of any age down to eight in their invasion of Lawrence, Kansas, he had struggled to recover. The war had been over when he arrived back at Slocum's Stand and had tried to pick up where his parents, both of whom had died during the war, had left off. His brother Robert had been killed during Pickett's Charge, leaving John Slocum the sole heir to about the finest land in all of Georgia. That was why a carpetbagger judge took a fancy to the rolling green hills, vast meadows, and farmland that had been in the family since King George

II had ceded it to the Slocums. No taxes had been paid, the judge had said. When he and a hired gunman had ridden out to take possession after a tax lien had been issued, they got more than they had bargained for.

They each got their own patch of land, six feet deep out by the springhouse. They had been worthless thieves, but that wasn't the way the law saw it. Killing judges was a serious crime, especially Reconstruction judges. Slocum had ridden away from his land and never looked back.

He had a wanted poster for murdering a judge on his head. Along the way, he had accumulated a few more for rustling and robbing.

He was hardly the most law-abiding of the four sitting at the table.

"I have a better idea. Let's talk business first," Slocum said. "That way you don't waste my time or your whiskey if I'm not interested."

"What makes you think we got a plan to—" Carbuncle clamped his mouth shut when he saw Laramie's glare. "Didn't mean to say that."

Slocum discounted both Kinsley and Carbuncle, and stared across the table at Laramie. Giving the man his due, he didn't wilt under Slocum's gaze.

"I knew there was more to you than a fast gun," Laramie said. "You don't mince words."

"Ten seconds," Slocum said, "then I'm leaving."

"The bank," Laramie said quickly. "We're gonna rob it and need a fourth to help."

Slocum was taken aback by the sudden revelation.

"And you said I didn't mince words," Slocum replied slowly. "Why me?"

"You didn't wear down that ebony handle on your six-gun polishin' it," Kinsley said. "You walked in, we knew right away you were what we need. A man who knows how to use his gun."

"And his head," Laramie added. "We're going to take down that bank across the street."

"Farmer's and Rancher's?" Slocum kept from laughing.

"That's the one. There're others in town, but they don't have a quarter of the money in 'em that Wilson's does," Kinsley said. "We have to be careful, but we kin rob it. We kin."

"You've been in the lobby, haven't you? You've seen the guards behind those metal plates?"

"We got that figgered real good," Carbuncle said eagerly. "Or Laramie does. He's real smart."

Slocum's mind raced. He wanted his money back. It would be fitting revenge on Wilson if he took the money with a considerable bit of interest, too.

"The banker's brother is the town marshal," Slocum said.

"We know all about him," Laramie said. "We don't have to worry none about Jethro Wilson. We get him drunker 'n a lord and he won't stir, even to tell his deputies what to do. Don't take much to get him likkered up, either."

"The man does like his booze," said Carbuncle.

"The guards in the bank?"

"We can take care of them easier than you think," Laramie assured him.

"They in cahoots?"

"Hell, no, we'd have to pay 'em. Those worthless hobbledehoys ain't willin' to die fer Wilson," said Kinsley. "We'll just make sure they got the choice."

"We know which they'll choose—running like scalded dogs or dying for Wilson," said Laramie.

Eight hundred dollars. The amount Wilson had swindled him out of kept coming back to Slocum. He wasn't going to get satisfaction—or his money—any other way.

"How much you looking to get in the robbery?" he asked.

"Well, sir, I reckon there's nigh on ten thousand dollars in that vault," said Laramie. "Might be more. We're lookin' at divvyin' up the money and having maybe three thousand each."

Slocum allowed as to how that was a good return for Wilson "borrowing" his money the way he had.

He reached for the whiskey bottle and poured himself a shot. It was time to listen to the rest of Laramie's scheme for emptying the bank's vault.

2

"You be ready, Slocum," said Laramie. The man looked positively pleased with his preparations for the robbery. Slocum had to admit *he* was, too. Laramie knew what it would take to crack open that hard nut of a bank and had everything ready to go.

That worried Slocum more than any opposition they might face from the guards in Wilson's bank. There was no reason for Laramie to invite him to join the robbery. Three men could handle it well, and a fourth was only going to take away an extra slice of the pie.

"You back up Carbuncle," Laramie ordered Slocum. "This is gonna be a cakewalk. Wait and see."

Slocum pulled up his water-soaked bandanna, as did Kinsley and Carbuncle. Laramie waited a little longer before following suit. He ignited two torches dipped in pine tar, handed one to Kinsley, then the pair took off across the street. Slocum led their horses to a spot to the side of the bank and waited with Carbuncle.

Carbuncle was nervous, but it was the kind of nerves a horse gets waiting for a race to start. He was eager, not frightened. This made Laramie's order to watch Carbuncle all the more peculiar. Then came shouts from inside the bank as huge gouts of black smoke billowed from the door-way. It was time to act.

Slocum and Carbuncle waited for the rush of customers and tellers to get out of the bank, then went in, guns drawn and ready. Slocum had to hand it to the guards. They stood their ground. Foolish though it was, they tried to do their duty. Both men hunkered down behind their metal shields, gagging and coughing at the heavy black smoke filling the lobby.

Eyes stinging, Slocum went to the first guard and helped him up.

"Out. The whole damn place's on fire," Slocum told him as he aimed the smoke-blinded man toward the door. The guard staggered off, leaving his rifle behind. A quick glance showed Carbuncle dealing with the other guard in a more direct fashion. He slugged the man on the side of the head, sending him facedown on the lobby floor.

Slocum nodded to Carbuncle, then joined Kinsley and Laramie in the rear of the bank. As he passed the president's desk, Slocum felt a jolt of anger. He wanted to fish his eight hundred dollars out of Wilson's wallet with his own fingers, but the president was nowhere to be seen.

"Give us a hand, will you?" called Kinsley. He struggled with four canvas bags. Slocum grabbed two and sagged under the weight.

"We got ourselves a passel of greenbacks," Laramie said, "but those bags are filled with gold coin."

Slocum hurried to leave. His eyes were burning now from the heavy pall, but breathing through his wet bandanna kept the smoke from his lungs. The torches Kinsley and Laramie had dropped in front of the tellers' cages showed no sign of going out. If anything, they produced even more of the heavy, choking black fumes. Outside, Slocum expected to run into their first real opposition. He was more surprised than disappointed when it didn't materialize.

A crowd was gathering across the street, but nobody appeared too eager to start a bucket brigade or call out the volunteer firemen to put out a fire. This suited Slocum just fine. Under the cover of the heavy clouds of smoke that hung all around, he got to his horse and heaved the two canvas bags over its rump. The horse protested such weight behind the saddle, but Slocum soothed it and started back.

He ran into the other three emerging, all lugging heavy crates or canvas bags.

"We got more 'n I'd hoped," Laramie said, gloating. "We might have robbed old Wilson of damn near fifty thousand!"

Slocum doubted they had made off with that much, but this was undeniably one of the smoothest, most profitable robberies he had ever seen—and he had seen plenty. He mounted, and they rode slowly down the alley beside the bank to the rear and then galloped from Austin.

"This is better 'n I'd planned," Laramie said as he kept his head down and pushed his horse even more. Slocum followed, wondering if they were heading to a hideout to divvy up the loot. That hadn't been mentioned, but he wasn't too worried. With the money he had in the two canvas bags, he could get by nicely for quite a spell if Laramie tried to double-cross him.

"Where're we goin'?" asked Carbuncle. "You never said, Laramie."

"That was in case the robbery didn't go so good," Laramie said, slowing to give his horse a rest. They were more than a mile beyond the fringes of Austin and heading to the northwest, into the Hill Country and its tangled undergrowth and dense thickets. Eluding any pursuit would be easy in such terrain.

"So, you got a place where we can rest up? The horses are starting to lather somethin' fierce," said Kinsley. His horse stumbled as it walked, already nearing exhaustion.

"Not too much farther. Might be I shoulda had fresh horses along the way, but it never occurred to me until now."

Slocum looked at Laramie sharply. Nothing got by

Laramie. He had thought of it and discarded the idea for some reason. Slocum turned wary.

"There it is, there!" cried Laramie, pointing. Ahead stood a tumbledown shack, partly hidden by tall, leafy sweet-gum trees. "We can rest up, then go our separate ways in the morning."

Slocum fell behind the other three as they went to the shack. He looked around for any sign that he was riding into a trap. The robbery had gone too smoothly. There was no reason for Laramie to invite Slocum to join them, even if there had been shooting. Maybe Laramie was a belt-and-suspenders man, not taking any undue risks, but Slocum wasn't buying it. Laramie had something in mind, but what it was Slocum couldn't say yet.

The other three had already dismounted, and fought to get their bags into the shack.

"You need help with those, Slocum?" Carbuncle scratched his butt as he watched Slocum slowly dismount. Slocum kept his horse between him and the cabin, just in case a gunman lay in wait.

"Could use a hand," Slocum allowed. He let Carbuncle wrestle one of the bags inside while he dragged the other. Pausing just inside the door caused Slocum to frown. He might have misread Laramie entirely. Stranger things had happened—but Slocum had never seen them.

The room was empty save for the three outlaws, a rickety table, and a couple of chairs.

"Hoist that bag up here on the table, Slocum. I want to get down to countin'," said Laramie. "You want to help divvy it?" Laramie looked at his two partners and snorted, "They don't count so good."

Slocum pulled up a chair and began counting. He put the greenbacks into four piles and Laramie worked on the gold coins. More than twenty minutes later, they had finished separating the take into equal portions.

"There you are, Slocum," Laramie said, pushing a stack

of gold double eagles and a pile of scrip toward Slocum. "I make that out to be more than four thousand dollars, paper and gold."

Kinsley and Carbuncle danced around, swinging each other first one way and then the other.

"We're rich, we're rich," they sang.

Laramie began stashing his cut into one of the canvas bags. He pointed to Slocum's money. "You want a bag for that? Here, take this one." Laramie had already loaded one from the bank and had placed it on the dirt floor. He pulled it back up and placed it on the table. "Easier to carry."

"Evidence of where it came from," Slocum pointed out. He started to open the bag and remove the money. His saddlebags would be adequate to carry such treasure. Laramie stopped him, half-standing, hand on Slocum's wrist.

Slocum pulled back, hand going for his six-shooter.

"Quiet," Laramie hissed. "You hear that? Horses! Somebody's already on our trail!"

"Texas Rangers!" Kinsley chanced a quick look outside through the partially opened door and ducked back in immediately. "There's a passel of 'em, too. A whole damn posse! What're we gonna do, Laramie?"

"We don't panic. Get your loot. We're goin' out the back."

Slocum grabbed the canvas bag and hoisted it to his shoulder. It was lighter than the one he had carried from the bank, but then there shouldn't have been a full amount of gold in it. Some paper money, some gold.

Laramie kicked out the boards in the rear of the cabin, looked around, then fumbled out a tin of lucifers. He began striking the matches, tossing them lit in all directions. The debris inside the shack caught on fire.

Slocum scraped through the hole Laramie had knocked in the wall as the interior of the shack exploded. The trio had already slung their loot over their horses and were heading deeper into the thicket. Slocum was a little slower getting his money secured, but he overtook the trio in nothing flat.

"You have another rendezvous?" Slocum asked.

"Don't matter. We each got our split. Head in any direction you like, and good luck." Laramie put his head down and rode deeper into the forest.

Slocum looked around for a decent escape route. It was getting dark and would be pitch black in a half hour. If he kept himself away from the posse that long, he could make his way across the border into Mexico in a few days of hard riding.

He followed a game trail, and then saw he had circled about and that Kinsley was riding along a crossing path. Slocum had started to call to the man and see if he knew a way through the heavily forested region when a shot rang out. Kinsley ducked low and tried to put his spurs to his horse's flanks. The horse bucked and threw him off. Hitting the ground hard, Kinsley tried to get up but collapsed, holding his leg.

Slocum had no liking for the man. He didn't have a dislike, either. He felt honor-bound to help because they had ridden together, even if it had been for such a short time.

Whooping and hollering, Slocum drew the attention of two men with the look of lawmen about them, although he didn't see tin badges pinned to their vests. Slocum should have ridden as hard and fast as he could, but he hesitated, drawing them from where Kinsley lay on the ground. The outlaw was smart enough to see what Slocum was doing and pressed himself low into the weeds. This wouldn't have worked if Slocum hadn't kept waving.

"This way," he shouted to the lawmen. "They went this way."

"Who the hell're you?" shouted the lawman in the lead. "You ain't in the posse."

"This way. They went this way. All of them!" Slocum wheeled his horse about and started riding, slowly to draw the two men after him. He didn't know if Kinsley would find his own horse and get to freedom, but he was getting a chance. More than that, Slocum couldn't provide.

Worse, he soon found that the deputies weren't all that slow understanding what was going on. They shouted and began shooting at him. Bullets whizzed past, ripping away leaves on low-hanging tree limbs. The gathering darkness favored Slocum with the chance to cut off the trail and blunder through the undergrowth a few yards, then go to ground. He dropped off the horse and gentled it to be sure it didn't whinny at the wrong time and bring the lawmen down on his head.

He saw two riders pass along the game trail he had taken, going deeper into the woods. He wasn't sure how long they would keep going before they gave up and returned to the main posse. Swinging into the saddle, Slocum backtracked to where Kinsley had fallen from his horse. He found tracks in the soft earth and trailed the outlaw almost a hundred yards before overtaking him.

"Give me your hand," Slocum said, reaching down to pull Kinsley up behind him.

"No, get on outta here, Slocum," Kinsley said. "There's a Ranger with the posse! I know him. He's chain lightning with a six-shooter and worse 'n glue if he gets on your trail."

"We can find your horse so you can ride. Your leg in bad shape?"

"Felt something snap in my knee when I fell. Hurts like hellfire, but I know these woods. You don't. Get outta here. Go!"

Kinsley sounded a mite desperate.

"What's going on?" Slocum asked. The expression on the outlaw's face told him something was wrong.

"You came back for me. You didn't have to do that, Slocum."

"We're partners, for the day, at least."

Kinsley shook his head, then pointed.

"Go on, get outta here. I'll be all right."

"What about your cut from the robbery?" Slocum

asked. "It's still in your saddlebags." Again Kinsley's expression didn't match what Slocum expected. Most men who had pulled off a bank robbery would be more concerned about their loot than their lives. That brand of greed had killed more than one outlaw. If Slocum had to bet on it, he would have thought Kinsley's greed would have exceeded his common sense. This didn't seem to be the case.

"It don't matter," came the surprising answer. "Gettin' away is all that matters."

"That must be one powerful tough hombre of a Ranger," Slocum said.

Kinsley stepped away from the side of Slocum's horse, turned, and limped away into the thicket. Sharp thorns cut at the man's hide, leaving his shirt and canvas pants in tatters. Then Kinsley vanished into the darkness as surely as if he had been swallowed by the very ground.

Slocum cocked his head to one side and listened hard. The usual sounds from a forest had quieted, letting him hear the steady clop-clop of horses' hooves coming this way. He had tried to fool two of the posse by claiming to be riding with them. That hadn't worked. What had worked was hiding. In the dark, Slocum stood a good chance of them passing him on the trail again.

He led his horse in the direction opposite to that taken by Kinsley, finding a spot behind a tree where he could see the shadowy trail. This time four lawmen rode along, two watching either side of the trail. Slocum hadn't thought they would be able to see much in the twilight, but at least one of the posse had eyes as good as any barn owl. He drew rein and pointed to the ground where Slocum had ridden away.

All four started in his direction. Slocum touched the butt of his six-shooter, and then worried that any shots fired would bring the rest down on him like flies to fresh cow flop. He walked his horse a short way until he found a break in the woods. A meadow stretched open and inviting.

Slocum swung into the saddle and got his horse trotting

steadily for the far side of the clearing. Before he reached the sanctuary of the forest ahead, a shot rang out. The slug missed him by a country mile, but was close enough to let him know the sharpshooter hadn't fired blindly. They had spotted him.

He got to the woods, changed direction, and cut to his right. By the time he had ridden another twisting, dodging ten minutes in the dark forest, he had no idea where he was headed. Not that it mattered. He only wanted to stay clear of the posse until they gave up and returned to Austin.

Blundering about in the undergrowth for another half hour brought him to a dual-rutted road. Enough wagon traffic passed this way to keep the weeds crushed and the dirt packed down hard. He considered riding along the road, but had no idea if he would be riding into the arms of the law or away. Rather than take a chance, he crossed the road and plunged into the dense forest on the far side.

As he made his way through the forest, he remembered what he had in his saddlebags. The loot from the robbery would convict him in a flash if the posse caught him. He should hide it somewhere—but where? He had no idea where he was and had no way of finding it again if he chose some decent place to stash it.

When he heard voices behind him, Slocum turned to grab the canvas bag with his share of the robbery loot in it. Better to dump it all and talk his way out of going to jail— or having a noose looped around his neck out here in the rolling hills of south Texas.

As he turned, his horse spooked. Slocum swung back to control the horse and felt a low tree limb smash into his skull. His head snapped back and Slocum fell to the ground, unconscious.

3

Slocum knew he wasn't dead. Dead couldn't possibly hurt this much. His head threatened to explode like a stick of dynamite and the pain every time he moved, no matter how slightly, set off new tremors in his body. He tried to reach to touch his forehead where the tree limb had smacked him, but for some reason his hands wouldn't work. He turned his head to one side and faced a bright light shining through his closed eyelids. Trying to speak produced only faint croaks from his throat, so he gave up.

Then he realized he was not alone. He heard two voices. Whoever they belonged to, they argued. As the buzzing in his ears died, he made out the voices better and caught the words.

A woman said, "You don't know what you're talking about."

A huskier voice, slower and with a decided Texas drawl: "Wall, you might have somethin' there, missy, but I need to find out."

"Do not call me that." The woman's voice carried a whip crack of command to it. Slocum struggled to place her accent and couldn't. He had heard it before, but his

19

head threatened to split in half and let his brains spill out if he tried to think too much more.

"He's comin' round, looks like," the man said.

Slocum gasped and thrashed about when water was dashed in his face. He got his hands moving this time to wipe the water from his eyes. He looked up into an almost full moon, turning the countryside into a liquid silver wonderland. It also caused the Ranger's badge to gleam as if it were on fire.

"What happened to you, mister?" the Ranger asked.

"Riding along. Hit my head in the dark."

"And where were you ridin' in the middle of the night?"

"Don't interrogate him that way, Ranger Coldcreek. He's hurt. Can't you see that?"

"You be quiet a spell, ma'am," the Ranger said. This time his voice carried a steel edge to it that shut the woman up.

Slocum propped himself up and got a good look at the woman for the first time. If his lips hadn't been chapped and his tongue dry, he would have let out a long, low wolf whistle. She was about the prettiest thing he had seen since coming to Texas, and he had seen mighty fine fillies. The woman was average height, but that was all that was ordinary about her. Square-cropped blond hair hung down to her shoulders. She wore a man's shirt better than any man ever could, filling it out to the bursting point. Trim waist, flaring hips, and a six-shooter holstered at her left side showed she preferred a cross-draw holster like Slocum did. She wore tight jeans with the tops stuffed into fancy hand-tooled boots. Everything about her reeked of money, but her attitude wasn't that of a spoiled rich girl.

"German," Slocum got out.

"*Eingeben ihm wasseren,*" she snapped, confirming it. Slocum looked from the Ranger back to the blond woman. She stood with balled hands on her hips, glaring at Slocum. Or was she giving the Ranger her full wrath?

Slocum gratefully accepted a canteen from the hands of

one of the posse, who mumbled something in German to the woman. Slocum was still a little shaky, but got most of the water dribbled across his lips and into his mouth. He felt better and could talk, but he knew he had better keep what he said to a minimum. The Ranger had the look of a vindicated lawman in his eyes. Ranger Coldcreek thought he had caught himself a bank robber.

"We need to take this varmint on back to Austin and ask a few questions, ma'am," the Ranger said.

"You'll do no such thing." She stamped her booted foot. Even in the moonlight Slocum saw the anger flashing in her eyes. "I can't spare him."

"Spare him? What are you sayin', ma'am?" asked the Ranger. "You know him?"

"He works for me. He's a hand on the Circle H. Ask my brother Uwe. He'll say the same."

"Don't reckon I could ask your pa, now could I?" Ranger Coldcreek took a step back when the woman swung at him. She missed his face, but not by much.

"Thanks," Slocum said loudly, holding up the canteen. The Ranger looked ready to swing back at her, but Slocum's gratitude defused the growing animosity. "That water hit the spot. I'll get on back to work, if you want," Slocum said, staring directly into the woman's bright blue eyes. "Or you want I should go with the posse?"

"You lazy oaf," she said, turning her anger on him. "You never have put in a solid day's work. I ask you to find the strays and you're off riding through the woods, probably to find someplace to sleep when you should be working. No, I don't want you to go into Austin. It's too far off."

"He's one of the robbers, Miss Helmann," the Ranger said. "We been trackin' the lot of 'em since Austin. Don't rightly know how many there was, but best guess is four."

"He doesn't do the work of one cowhand, much less four," the blonde said. "You can have him if I can borrow a couple of your posse to do his chores."

"A couple? Why a couple?"

"To make up for the work he hasn't been doing while he's sitting there on his butt!"

"You sure he works for you?" asked the Ranger. Before the woman could say anything, Coldcreek amended, "You have him on your payroll. Don't much care if he is doin' much work, long as you vouch for him."

"I do that, *ya*," the woman said. Her slip into German told Slocum she was lying, but the Ranger missed the small nervous change into her native language. Or maybe he wanted to discount it. Believing a woman as attractive as this one came easy to a man on the Texas range whose only companion was likely to be his horse at the best of times and a posse of smelly men at others.

"Mount up, boys," the Ranger called. "We still got bank robbers to run to ground." Coldcreek turned to the woman, touched the brim of his hat, and said, "Much obliged for settin' me straight the way you did, ma'am. Sometimes I forget my manners when duty calls, as it's doin' loud and clear right now."

"Get on, Ranger. Get on after those robbers."

Slocum got to shaky feet and wobbled a mite when dizziness hit him. He touched his forehead. A lump the size of a hen's egg had sprouted and was tender to the touch.

"You cracked your pate well and good," she said.

"How's that?"

"You smashed your head, *dummkopf*."

"Reckon so," Slocum said. He looked hard at her and asked, "Why'd you tell the posse I worked for you?"

"I have no liking for the Ranger and less for those men riding with him," she said. "They—never mind."

"My name's Slocum. John Slocum."

"Gretchen Helmann," she said, shoving her hand out. Slocum shook. As he expected, Gretchen's grip was as strong and sure as any man's.

"Miss Helmann," he said, wondering if he ought to ask the question burning on his tongue. "How do you know I'm not one of the robbers the Ranger's after?"

She shrugged her shapely shoulders. Slocum's mind drifted for a moment when he saw the play of cloth over her chest; then he came back to the important question. She had saved him from jail or maybe a noose.

"I found you before they did. You've been knocked out for more than twenty minutes."

"That long," Slocum marveled. If he had guessed, he would have thought it was only a few seconds.

"I found you, and they rode up and we spent at least ten minutes arguing; then you awoke."

"That doesn't answer how you know I'm not a robber."

"I looked through your saddlebags," she said. "For something to help you. When I left the house this morning, I did not bring things for cleaning wounds or binding them. Your head is bleeding."

He gingerly touched the swollen spot, and his fingers came away sticky.

"I searched your saddlebags," Gretchen went on, "and found nothing to say you are a robber."

Slocum's eyes darted to the canvas bag slung on the rump of his horse. It didn't carry markings from the bank, but it held his share of the loot. Gretchen turned to see what he stared at.

"You are a strange robber, if that is what you steal," she said. Seeing his confusion, Gretchen dragged the canvas bag down and opened it. She pulled out a sheaf of paper. "Who steals the *Houston Triweekly Gazette,* all cut up and put into nice stacks?"

"What?" Slocum grabbed the sheaf from her hands and stared at the newsprint. He flipped through the stack and then cursed. Laramie had double-crossed him back at the cabin. Kinsley had called out that the posse was closing in at exactly the right instant. When Slocum had looked away, Laramie made the switch. One canvas bag looked like any other. Slocum took the bag and upended it. Rocks fell to the ground.

"So? Cut-up newspaper and worthless rocks," Gretchen

said. "You are surprised to see this? Your partners double-crossed you?"

"Are you going to call the Ranger back?"

"You could stop me," she said in a low voice. "Would you do that?" Before he could answer, a small smile curled the corners of her mouth. "No, you would not do this. You are a gentleman, in spite of your rough exterior." Her bright blue eyes dropped to the worn ebony handle on his Colt Navy. "You are a gentleman and a gunman, yes?"

"What if I rode off?" Slocum asked.

"It might be necessary to find Ranger Coldcreek and tell him you threatened me. But would he believe me?"

"You could charm the stars right out of the sky," Slocum said. His answer took her by surprise. Her mouth opened, then shut abruptly.

"You are a gentleman, yes."

"And I can use the six-gun," Slocum admitted.

"You . . . you must help me now that I have helped you." Gretchen tried to keep the note of desperation from her words, but failed. "We must ride. Get away from the posse."

"Ride where?" Slocum was itching to get on Laramie's trail and retrieve his share of the robbery money. Since he had come to Texas, he had been cheated by a crooked banker and an equally crooked bank robber. Slocum knew he had been a perfect sucker for Laramie's scheme. They'd robbed the bank, Laramie had foisted off nothing but cut newsprint and rocks, then the Ranger and the posse had found him. The lawmen would have someone to pin the robbery on and take away the heat Wilson was likely to put on them—and Laramie, with his two partners, would have a safe place to hide. Laramie hadn't been joking when he said he had planned this well.

Robbery, someone to take the fall, a place to hide where the posse would never find him. Perfect.

"It would be a shame to call the Ranger," Gretchen said, seeing the resolve in him to go after Laramie, Kinsley, and

Carbuncle. "You would not hurt me." She sounded less sure of this, but he saw that she reached for the pistol slung in its holster.

"I don't hurt women," he said, "unless they throw down on me. That puts them the equal of any man."

Her hand moved away from her six-shooter.

"That is fair," Gretchen said. "I have a camp not far off. We must talk this through."

Slocum found himself more than a little curious about the lovely blond German woman. She was in her late twenties and as cute as a button, but she acted as if she rode alone. Slocum found it hard to believe she didn't have a husband and a gaggle of kids tugging on her apron strings.

They rode in silence through the forest until they reached a clearing. Gretchen had pitched her camp at the edge. There was a cold fire pit, some gear, and nothing more. Somehow, Slocum had expected to see a husband waiting, and it surprised him that Gretchen rode through the Hill Country alone.

"Why're you out here?" he asked.

"Here? This is Circle H property," she said. "I need to ride it now and again to see what it is we own."

Slocum heard more in her words, but didn't pursue the question. He was more interested in finding out why she had saved him from the Ranger. There was little doubt he was one of the men the posse had been hunting.

"Start a fire," she said. "I'll get some coffee brewing then."

Slocum found some twigs and heavier deadwood, piled them into the pit, and spent a few minutes working with lucifers from his tin to get the fire going. It felt good in the growing night chill. He warmed his hands and thought how it would be even warmer with Gretchen alongside. But she was closed off to him, her body tense and her hand seldom straying from the butt of her six-shooter. He had no doubt she could use it, too.

Gretchen brewed the coffee, poured a cup, and finally got around to her reason for saving him.

"I need help," she said straight out. Her blue eyes fixed on him over the rim of her tin coffee cup.

"You own a big spread," Slocum said. "You must have plenty of hands who could rope and brand cattle."

"It's complicated, what I need," she said. "My pa . . ." She struggled to find the words.

"He in trouble?"

"Big trouble," Gretchen said. "They have him locked up."

"The Ranger?"

"Oh, no, worse than that. He's in the Breiland Institute for the Insane."

This took Slocum aback.

"He's crazy?"

"No! It's all part of a plot to grab the Circle H. They have him locked up and he's not crazy and he has to get out. I want to get him out, and I can't ask just anybody."

"You said you had a brother. What's he doing to help?"

Gretchen turned positively cold. She tossed away her mostly untasted coffee and glared at Slocum.

"Uwe put him there. He is the one stealing the ranch!"

"The law can't help? There's got to be a judge or—" Slocum bit off the rest of his protest. Gretchen wasn't a flighty little hothouse flower who didn't understand how things worked in the real world. It looked as if her brother had this angle covered and must have bought off a judge to have their father committed.

"Get him out. Break him out, shoot the bastards holding him, I don't care what has to be done. But get him out before Uwe gets final legal control of the ranch. When that happens, there won't be any reason to keep Papa alive." She sucked in a deep breath and let it out in a gusty sigh. "Or me," she added. "There won't be any reason to keep me alive, either."

Slocum sipped at his coffee. It was bitter, but he didn't

expect much else out on the trail, and Gretchen had not put much effort into improving the taste.

"Get him out of that hellhole," she said, the stern determination coming into her words. "Peter Helmann. Get him out. Shoot them all if you have to, but get him out." Gretchen paused a moment, then added, "It would be good if you shot them as you get him out. They are evil and should die."

"Why'd I want to go doing this killing for you? And rescuing your pa?"

Gretchen hardened even more.

"You robbed that bank in Austin. I do not know why you had only rocks and that cut-up *Houston Triweekly Gazette,* but I recognized the bag they were in. It is a bank bag."

Slocum locked eyes with her and saw she was not bluffing.

"What keeps me from gunning you down and riding on my way? If I'm such a desperado, that's what I'd do."

"You are a gentleman. You do not kill women, but you should kill—" Gretchen bit off her sentence. "You will get him out of there. Peter Helmann. Remember the name."

"I've got a good memory," Slocum allowed.

"Here is a map showing you the way to the Breiland Institute for the Insane." She fumbled about inside her shirt and pulled out a folded sheet of paper. Slocum took it and tilted it to the fire to see the penciled map. It took him a few seconds to orient the paper to get an idea where he was.

"How do I find you after I get him out?"

"He knows how to get back to the ranch house. That is where I shall be."

Slocum tucked the paper into his own shirt.

"You're taking a big chance on me," he said.

He was rewarded with a tiny smile and a shake of her head that set her short blond hair moving like tall grass in the wind.

"I do not think this is so. You will get Papa out safe and sound. I know it."

"From the look of the map, I can reach the place before sunup if I ride now." He got to his feet. Gretchen looked up at him, her blue eyes softer than before.

"Danke," she said.

Slocum didn't trust himself to say anything more to Gretchen Helmann since he had no intention of finding this nuthouse or rescuing her father. He was going after Laramie and his two partners. As he rode into the darkness of the forest, Slocum felt his ire rising like a chilly night wind. He had risked his own neck to save Kinsley, and the man was part of the scheme to double-cross him.

Kinsley would pay. So would Carbuncle. And Slocum would find something particularly appropriate to do to Laramie.

He cut through the forest, circled a while, and came out on a road leading to the northwest. Laramie had been heading in this direction, and Slocum thought the others were intent on joining their boss by the way they had high-tailed it when Ranger Coldcreek showed up at the shack. What Slocum didn't know was if the Ranger was in cahoots with Laramie and had appeared on cue like some actor in a bad play, or if he had only run them to ground at that exact instant.

As far as it went, Laramie couldn't have picked a better time for his switch of gold and greenbacks for worthless dross.

"The *Houston Triweekly Gazette,*" Slocum scoffed as he rode. Houston was where Laramie had come from. Slocum remembered that detail from something the outlaw had said back in Austin. Making Laramie eat every scrap of that paper before getting a slug in the gut might not be enough, but Slocum thought it was a start.

A slow smile came to Slocum's lips when he saw fresh hoofprints in the soft earth. He dismounted, pressed his cheek to the ground, and studied the tracks a few minutes, getting every detail of the horseshoe with a large nick in its side firmly in mind. He could follow this horse to the ends

of the earth—and he was positive he had found the outlaws' trail when two other horses joined the first on the
road.

Slocum pictured them perfectly in his head. He touched
his Colt Navy and knew the six shots in the cylinder would
be enough to put two slugs in each of them. He swung back
in the saddle and urged his tired horse onward faster. The
Ranger and his posse were out in the countryside somewhere. It wouldn't do to let the Ranger catch Laramie first.

Even seeing Laramie swinging from a tall oak wouldn't
satisfy Slocum. He wanted justice to come from his own
six-gun.

The tracks never strayed from the road. Slocum trotted
along as the sun began poking up over the wooded area on
his right. Then he pulled back on the reins and simply
stared. The road ended ahead—and Laramie and his gang
had ridden in there.

Slocum was at the front gate of the Breiland Institute for
the Insane.

4

"If this don't beat all," Slocum muttered to himself. He fished out the map Gretchen had given him, smoothed it in front of him on the saddle, and studied it. Without knowing it—by following Laramie—he had ridden straight to the front gates of the Breiland Institute for the Insane.

Slocum tucked the map back into the front of his shirt and stared at the stark, forbidding place. A high rock wall circled the grounds, overrun with weeds and tangles of thistle. On top of the wall ran a strand of rusty barbed wire. The three-story brick buildings sadly needed scrubbing. Soot and other debris clung to the walls, turning the entire structure into a black castle of sorts. Turrets rose at the two front corners. In one hung a bell. In the other Slocum thought he saw a man moving about. The rising sun glinted off metal. Possibly a guard with a rifle stood watch up there, ready to take a shot at any inmate trying to escape.

To Slocum's dismay, the iron gates were swung wide open. If this were supposed to be inviting, it failed.

As he sat and studied the Institute grounds, two more guards appeared. Both of them wore white coats and carried buffalo rifles capable of knocking over a woolly at a hundred yards. At this range, they could blow Slocum clean in half. This decided him on what to do. He sat a little straighter in the saddle and urged his horse into the unkempt grounds.

They had seen him, the road ended here, why rouse suspicions? A million other items flashed though Slocum's mind, but taking the bull by the horns was his safest course of action from the interest the guards were showing him now.

As he dismounted in front of tall double oak doors, he got a better look at the one tower. He had not been mistaken. A guard in the tower peered down at him—sighting along the barrel of his rifle.

"Howdy," Slocum greeted the two guards coming over to him. One approached from the front while the other stayed to one side as if they wanted to keep him in a cross fire. Which they probably did.

"You got business here, mister?" asked the guard in front of him. He might wear a white jacket, but Slocum saw that he was no doctor. His fingernails were broken and grimy; he had a bright gold tooth in front and scars on his face that came from knife fighting. For all the man's battered condition, he fixed a steely look on Slocum. And his finger never strayed from the trigger of his .60-caliber Sharps.

"Reckon so," Slocum said, "but it's kind of private. I'd like to speak with the director." He worried that this might cause the guards to shoot him out of hand. Instead, they relaxed and the one with the gold tooth even laughed. It wasn't a hearty laugh—it carried more than a little hint of menace.

"You come to the right place, mister. Jesse there'll see you in to talk with the doc."

"The door's open," Jesse said. "Ya go right on in, and I'll foller ya."

Slocum handed the horse's reins to Gold Tooth, got an even bigger leer, and went to the towering oak doors. He pushed on one door and it swung inward on oiled hinges.

Inside the Institute building he found a long flagstone-paved corridor leading to the depths of the building off the cathedral-like lobby. A staircase swung around on his right, and to the left along the wall stretched a row of doors.

"Git yerse'f on in that second door, mister," the guard said. The man pointed with his left hand. Slocum saw that he never took his right away from the stock and rested the barrel on his left arm in such a way that he could fire.

Slocum hesitated in front of the door, wondering if he ought to go in. He knocked and heard a muffled "Enter."

The room was lavishly furnished with wing-back chairs placed near a large fireplace. Two walls were floor-to-ceiling bookcases, and the rug on the floor in front of the massive wooden desk had to be Oriental from the writhing dragon pattern woven into it. Seated behind the desk, peering over wire-rimmed glasses, was about the homeliest man Slocum had ever seen. His first impression was that of a weasel, but that was something of an insult to weasels.

"May I help you, sir?" The man rose. He was shorter than Slocum expected and oddly proportioned. He came around the desk with a curious gait that hinted at some leg injury. A head too big for his body, a leg that trailed the other perceptibly, a hand thrust out that was mostly bone. Slocum shook the outthrust hand with some distaste.

"I was recommended to this place," he started. "I'm not sure I got to the right spot, though."

"Why did you seek out the Breiland Institute for the Insane?"

"That's kind of personal," Slocum said, trying to find the proper excuse that wouldn't bring the guards down on his neck.

"You're not, shall we say, running *from* something, are you?"

Slocum thought that was a strange question. He shook his head.

"You might say it's just the opposite of that. I'm running to something."

"Then you've found the right place." The man smiled. Slocum wished he hadn't. He had perfect, white teeth that looked more like sharp spikes. "I am Dr. Poston, the director of this Institute. Allow me to show you the way, since my assistant is otherwise indisposed."

"I wouldn't want to put you out, Doctor," Slocum said. He got an increasingly bad feeling and wanted to back out now. Taking his chances with the armed guards was better than staying here with this ghoulish man. He understood gunfights and lead bullets. He had no idea what he was being led into by Dr. Poston.

"Oh, don't be shy, sir. A man of your, umm, build and undoubted experience should never be shy, especially in an establishment such as this. Might I ask how you heard of the Institute's offerings?"

"Word gets around," Slocum said. "Might have heard mention of it in a saloon," he added when he saw his first vague answer wasn't going to suit the director. For whatever reason, saying that he had learned of the Institute in a saloon assuaged the director's curiosity when it ought to have inflamed it. What would Slocum have overheard in a saloon about a crazy house that would have brought him out to the middle of the Hill Country to find it?

"Yes, yes, that is so. We must not be too talkative about the Institute, however, since we wouldn't want to ruin the finer aspects of it." The doctor opened the office door back into the lobby and pointed up the stairs.

"Third floor. You will enjoy the view, I am sure."

Slocum started up the stairs since Dr. Poston watched him like a snake studies a bird. There was a mutual wariness and obvious danger, but Slocum couldn't figure what danger Poston thought he might be in surrounded by guards and a veritable fortress.

"A moment, sir. That will be twenty dollars."

Slocum started to ask for what, then decided he would be in hot water if he questioned the doctor. He found some greenbacks stuffed into his shirt pocket. He peeled off four fives and handed them over.

"I see you are a man of discernment. Many protest the cost, but it is worth it, sir, well worth it! Now hurry, up the stairs. Your destiny awaits!"

Slocum wanted to bolt and run, but Dr. Poston remained in the doorway of his office, beady dark eyes fixed on him. Slocum went to the stairs and stopped counting when he reached thirteen—the number leading to a gallows. He was only halfway to the second floor, but was already out of sight from anyone below due to the extreme curvature. He rested his hand on the butt of his six-gun, but saw nothing to cause any alarm. The stairway had small tables every few steps with small statues of naked women on them. The paintings on the walls were also more likely to be seen behind a bar at better saloons. If nothing else, Slocum liked the doctor's taste in decoration, even if it struck him as odd for a place where loco people were locked up.

He passed the second-floor corridor. A long way toward the end, a single door stood open. He considered going to see what was beyond, but he heard voices from the third floor. Laughter. He took the steps two at a time to reach the third floor. At the top he simply stared.

He had left the Hill Country of Texas and walked into a New Orleans brothel. Red velvet wallpaper, the furnishings, the paintings on the walls, even more erotically explicit statues than he saw on the way up—it matched any whorehouse he had ever been in.

"Would you care for a drink?" The voice was low and husky and utterly female. He turned and saw a woman dressed only in bloomers and a corset rise from a chair where she had been seated, obviously waiting for him. Or whoever had come up the stairs.

She was a short redhead with a considerable amount to try to stuff down behind that corset.

"You like, eh?" She pushed her hands up under her breasts, making them seem even larger. "For such a small thing, I have big things, eh?"

"Lovely," Slocum said. The soft shuffle of bare feet caused him to look into the room opening off the head of the stairs. A half-dozen women in various stages of undress came from rooms that had been hidden behind screens and wall hangings.

"*Da*, we are luffly," said a sultry voice. The woman came to him. She was dressed in a floor-length ball gown. At the bodice were pearls sewn cunningly to accentuate the tops of her snowy-white breasts. He knew her accent wasn't German, but he couldn't place it immediately.

"I am Ludmilla," she said. "I once was the Czar's consort."

The other women, including the one who had greeted him, hung back. This told Slocum who was in charge of this whorehouse.

"The Czar has terrible taste," Slocum said. A black cloud crossed Ludmilla's face as anger seized her.

"You choose one of *them*?" She spit out the word as if it were a curse.

"You misunderstand," Slocum said. "I meant that the Czar had terrible judgment if he let a lovely flower such as yourself out of his sight, much less his country."

Ludmilla laughed, pulled out a fan, and opened it. She fanned herself furiously and coyly looked at him over the rim.

"You toy with Ludmilla," she said. In a whisper she added, "You may toy with Ludmilla more."

Slocum considered what to do. She wasn't anywhere near the prettiest of the women, but was obviously the madam. That meant she had information Slocum needed. He couldn't turn around and go back down the stairs without causing a commotion that would bring the guards with their long rifles running. If he did anything out of the ordinary, he would make himself a target.

It wasn't hard figuring out how to fit in.

"Do you have a room? I would escort you there," Slocum said.

"You are such a gentleman," Ludmilla said, plainly delighted. She held out her arm. Slocum took it, as if he led her to the grand ballroom and presentation to the Czar of all Russia. She steered him through the furniture in the room toward the rear, where a spiral iron staircase curled upward. He had not seen this turret from below since it was located directly in the middle of the Institute and would have been hidden from him.

She preceded him up the stairs, and Slocum got a tantalizing view of her trim ankle and shapely legs as she made her way up. He hung back and verified what he suspected. She reached the top of the stairs, turned, and lifted her skirts. Unlike the other soiled doves who wore bloomers, Ludmilla had nothing on under her skirts.

Slocum found himself responding, even as he told himself he was here to find Peter Helmann and not to dally. Somehow, he convinced himself a dalliance now would get him the information he needed. But later.

He went up the spiral stairs one step at a time, taking in the view. He lost sight of Ludmilla's smiling face when he got almost to the top and she threw her skirts out over his head. He was plunged into darkness, but felt the heat from her legs and above. Homing in on this, he kissed one silky-smooth inner thigh and worked his way up slowly. By the time he got to the moist nest between her legs, she was trembling.

"A Continental man, *da*," Ludmilla said in a voice entirely different from the one she had used below. The Russian accent was apparent, but the pitch was higher. He felt her hands pressing into the back of his head through layers of skirt. His tongue flashed out and raked up and down, tasting salty goodness and then plunging forward. This robbed Ludmilla of all strength. He had to reach up and cup her buttocks as she sank down. He followed her, lavishing kisses and licking furiously as she reached the floor and raised her knees high.

The skirts slid away from Slocum's head and revealed her face, a mask of ecstasy on it. He had seldom found a woman who responded so powerfully and quickly.

"Do not stop. *Nyet, nyet,* not to stop!"

She pushed down her bodice and let twin mounds pop out. In the sunlight slanting through etched glass windows, Slocum saw the cherry-red nubs atop each breast begin to harden with lust. They popped up even more when Ludmilla took them between thumb and forefinger and began rolling them about.

"That's my job," Slocum said. "But I won't use my fingers." He scooted up between her legs enough to press his mouth down on her left teat. The marshmallowy mound sagged under his oral assault. He rolled the nipple about with only the tip of his tongue; then he closed his lips around it and sucked. Hard. This brought the woman up off the floor as she tried to cram her entire teat into his face. He didn't want to let her control what was happening. Slocum had the gut feeling that would kill any chance he had of learning from her what he needed to know.

He lifted his head as she arched her back and let the slippery button of flesh pop from his lips.

"*Nyet,* no!" she pleaded.

Slocum dived down on the other breast, giving it his full attention. This produced more sobs of joy from the woman, but he wasn't content with the tongue-lashing he was giving her. He licked all around the sensitive tip, then slid down into the deep valley between her breasts so that his tongue left a broad wet streak wherever it went. Face buried between those glorious fleshy mountains, he kissed and licked and began lightly nipping. Every love bite brought new cries of pleasure to Ludmilla's lips.

As his mouth worked, so did his hands. Slocum got his

gun belt off, and then didn't waste any more time with his own clothing. He ran his hands under her skirts, pushing them up around her waist to expose her nether lips. His middle finger sailed into her warm, damp interior and wiggled about. Coupled with the action of his tongue, he controlled her totally.

This went on for several minutes until Slocum could no longer stand it. He was trapped in his tight jeans and every passing minute was more painful for him. Rocking back and coming up to his knees, he started to unbutton the fly.

"That is *my* job," Ludmilla said, eyes feverish with lust. She sat up, legs spread wide so they went along the floor on either side of Slocum. The Russian woman unfastened the buttons with practiced ease and let his long, hard shaft snap out. For only a moment was it all by itself in the cool air of the woman's aerial love nest. She dived on it, took the purpled arrowhead into her mouth, and began using her tongue in skilled ways that sent lightning bolts of pure lust throughout Slocum's loins.

For a few seconds, the sheer overwhelming joy of her mouth working so diligently on his manhood robbed him of speech. Then he laced his fingers through her jet-black hair and moved her mouth away.

"You're too good. I'm not a young buck with his first woman, but that's the way you make me feel."

"Make *me* feel!"

Slocum ran his hands up and down Ludmilla's legs, feeling the smooth flesh ripple at his touch. He grabbed a double handful of fleshy ass and lifted powerfully as he turned. Her leg swung up and around him so she ended up belly-down on the floor. Not content with this, Slocum snaked his hands under her waist and lifted her to hands and knees, her proud behind presented for him.

He moved forward and felt his fleshy staff slip between those meaty half-moons and then go lower. He thrust, but missed his target. She put her cheek against the floor and reached back between her legs and caught at him with her questing fingers. He gasped as those fingers stroked over his length and the hairy sac dangling beneath, then guided him directly to the spot they both wanted hit.

He felt her inner warmth surround his tip. He moved forward an inch and she gasped. Slowly, teasingly, he advanced an inch at a time until he was fully hidden away in the steamy, moist female sheath. Her entire body shook in reaction to his gentle intrusion. Slocum reared up and shoved himself fractions of an inch deeper, reveling in the tightness and warmth seeping into his steely hard shaft.

"*Da*, yes, more. I want more!" she cried. Her hips thrust back into the curve of Slocum's groin. They fit together perfectly. He leaned forward and stroked over her dangling breasts. His fingers caught at first one nip and then the other, milking her like he would a cow. The flesh snapped back into place every time he released it—and Ludmilla's arousal grew.

Slocum had wanted to prolong this, but every time she tensed strong inner muscles, it sent a new quake of desire pounding throughout his loins. He was on fire and had to move.

He began pulling back. Her muscles clamped down hard, trying to prevent his retreat. But once he was almost all the way out, only the thick head remaining between those fleshy pink curtains, he reversed course. Faster this time. Harder. He felt friction between his entire length and her inner tissue.

Ludmilla gasped and sobbed and began rotating her hips as he came and went from her tightness. They worked together well. Her movement coupled with his drove both their passions to the breaking point. She gasped and shuddered like a leaf in a high wind. Then he began flying like a shuttlecock back and forth so fast that he no longer had control. His desires ruled.

And he spilled his seed within her clutching interior. As he blasted forth, lava-hot, she shuddered all over again. Then Ludmilla sank to the cool floor. Her body looked as if it had been seized with a palsy. She continued to shake until Slocum thought something was wrong.

She rolled onto her side, showing him one naked breast and a big smile.

"Seldom have I felt such ecstasy," she said in a sex-husky voice. "I should pay you."

"But you won't," Slocum guessed.

"But no, *nyet,* that is not the way of this country," she said. "You would not haff it another way, eh?"

Slocum wasn't sure what Ludmilla meant. Then he found out. It cost him another twenty, but it was even more a bargain considering her skilled, knowing ways.

5

"You've got quite a view from up here," Slocum said, buttoning his fly and then settling his six-shooter at his waist. He peered through the etched glass. It distorted what he saw, but he got a better idea of the layout of the Breiland Institute for the Insane than before. The wall around the Institute blocked some of the spots where he suspected armed men patrolled.

"I had quite the view, *da,*" Ludmilla said, leaning back on a fainting couch. Her hungry eyes worked up and down his body, but stopped at his crotch. "You hide my view, you naughty boy."

"You want another view, you'll have to pay me," Slocum said. He saw a momentary flash across her face, as if she might actually take him up on this offer. Then basic greed dictated, outpacing lust.

"I do not choose for my own many of those who come here," Ludmilla said, her voice more heavily accented now than before. "But you. I choose you anytime."

"That's mighty inviting," Slocum said. He moved around the tower room, seeing more guards patrolling below. "But having so many men with rifles makes me uneasy about coming back again."

"You come anytime. I make you," she said. Then, as if she finally understood what he had meant: "They are needed, those guards. We have crazy men here. Everywhere crazy men."

Slocum had to admire whoever had thought of putting a whorehouse in the same spot as an insane asylum. They would never be bothered by lawmen wanting to fine them or take a significant cut of the girls' money. Whatever was paid here stayed here. He wondered if Ranger Coldcreek even knew Ludmilla ran this place.

Or was this entirely Ludmilla's house of ill repute?

"Is he really a doctor?"

"Dr. Poston? *Da*, he is. He takes care of them." Her pert nose wrinkled a little as she referred to the inmates.

"Could I see them? The men locked up here?"

"The men? You want to see only the men?"

"You have women inmates, too?"

"Some visitors find them even more appealing than me and my ladies," Ludmilla said. "I do not understand this. Those bitches are crazy. Mine are skilled."

Slocum sucked in his breath and held it for a moment. The Institute was even stranger than he had expected.

"The crazies I see mostly end up with a bullet in their guts," he said. "Who gets locked up here?"

"*Da*, some villages keep their insane ones as pets," Ludmilla said. "Here we get ones who are not pets."

Slocum waited to see if she would offer to show him around. He doubted anyone got into the wings radiating outward like spokes in a wheel from this central tower without being challenged by guards. From the number he saw on the grounds, there had to be even more inside. Escape was possible, but the guards had to maintain discipline inside, even if the inmates were in straitjackets or locked in cells.

"You do not want to see that," Ludmilla said confidently. "You want to see this." She lifted her skirts and flashed him a quick glimpse of a darkly furred triangle nestled between her thighs. As quickly as she lifted her skirts, she dropped them. She was one hell of a salesman peddling her goods.

"I've got more money," Slocum said, "but no more stamina. You plumb wore me out."

"I do not believe," Ludmilla said. "You are big and strong. You haff the vigor to go all night, and it is only midday."

Slocum shook his head.

"Then you go and return when you haff rested. Ask for me. I will claw out the eyes of anyone else who tries to lure you into her bed!"

With this pronouncement, Ludmilla got to her feet and motioned for him to precede her down the spiral staircase. Slocum went slowly, taking in all the details of the Institute he could. The room below where he had seen the other Cyprians was deserted. He had to wonder where the trade came from to keep so many ladies occupied. They were miles from any town, and the road ended at the front gate. It wasn't as if they serviced a stagecoach stopover or a train station.

"Go, keep going," Ludmilla said, shooing him along. He went back down to the ground floor and turned in time to see two guards moving a shackled man down a hallway. A heavy door slammed behind them.

"Was that a crazy?" he asked. "I'd like to see one up close." He was halfway down the hallway to the door before Ludmilla let out a squeak that meant for him to stop. Slocum didn't. He opened the door and looked into a dingy room with a chair in the middle. The man was chained in that chair, and one guard held a short length of knotted rope. From the marks on the man's face, the guard had laid the rope across his cheek and forehead a time or two.

"Come, go, you are not here wanted," Ludmilla said, grabbing his arm and pulling him back. She shot the guards a dark look and kept pushing Slocum toward the front doors. Dr. Poston came from his study. Slocum saw the man had a hand hidden in a coat pocket. From the way he stood, Poston clutched a small pistol.

"What's going on, Ludmilla?"

"Nothing, Doctor, nothing. He just leaving." Ludmilla kept pushing Slocum toward the doors. This time he let her shove him into the sultry Hill Country afternoon.

Two guards came up immediately, both waving their rifles around. Before he could ask about his horse, Gold Tooth brought it. The guard silently handed Slocum the reins.

Slocum turned to say good-bye to Ludmilla, but she had ducked back into the Institute entryway.

"You get a good tour?" asked Gold Tooth.

"Reckon I got a real good one," Slocum said. Then the guard said something that Slocum didn't understand.

"You come on back and stay, when you have to."

Slocum nodded and rode through the open gates and retraced his path to the point in the road where he had last spotted Laramie and his partners' tracks. He drew rein and stared at them. The tracks definitely led into the Institute. Had they hired on as guards? That struck him as wrong. Laramie wasn't the kind to take orders from anybody, and all the guards were well disciplined, walking their patrols like Army sentries. From what little he had seen, Ludmilla controlled her part of the Institute with an iron hand and Dr. Poston controlled her.

Laramie would never take orders from a snake in the grass like Poston.

Slocum got out of sight of the Institute guards, then made a wide circuit of the grounds. It took him the rest of the day to circumnavigate the buildings, and nowhere else did he find a gate or even a break in the wall. Laramie, Kinsley, and Carbuncle had ridden in, and there was no sign they had ever left.

Might be they had hired on as guards like the pair beating up the inmate, but this didn't set well with Slocum, either. It went against everything he had learned about the trio.

Night falling, he got back on the road and doubled back to where he had left Gretchen Helmann the night before. He wasn't sure she would have remained in one spot, but she had. She was on her feet and coming toward him as he crossed the meadow.

The moon hadn't risen yet, and her face was completely hidden in shadow. Still, he felt her tension and knew how she looked.

"What did you find? You didn't return with Papa." She made it sound as if he had failed.

"Didn't see him, didn't try to find him. That place is better protected than most Army forts," he said. "You got any of that coffee? Or something to eat? I'm so hungry my belly's rubbing up against my backbone." He tried to remember when he had last eaten and couldn't. It had been before the bank robbery back in Austin. Since then he had been constantly on the go, running from Texas Rangers, tracking double-crossers—and getting laid in a Texas insane asylum.

It had been alternately nerve-racking and enjoyable. And now he was hungry.

"You did not find him? But he's in there! He has to be! That's where Uwe was told they'd take him."

"Let's talk this out," Slocum said, going to where Gretchen had built a small fire. He thrust out his hands and felt the warmth easing some of the aches.

"I have some sausage and bread."

"That'll be mighty fine," Slocum said. He sank down to a spot in the grass beside the fire and let Gretchen fetch the food for him. He couldn't remember being more tired, but he still found the energy to eat what she handed him. He appreciated her restraint in not interrogating him until the bread and meat sat comfortably in his belly. He washed it all down with some of her bitter coffee.

"Here's what I saw," he said finally, picking his teeth with the tip of the knife drawn from the sheath in the top of his boot. He told her about the layout of the Breiland Institute for the Insane and meeting Dr. Poston. He didn't go into detail about how he had spent his morning with Ludmilla when he saw Gretchen looking at him with more than a touch of resentment. Slocum had to wonder if the blonde didn't like him taking time off from hunting for her pa or if it was something else, something more possessive on her part.

"You did not see him? My papa?"

Slocum shook his head, then said, "I did see something mighty strange, though. Two guards were beating up a man who didn't look like he belonged in an insane asylum."

"They must discipline the inmates," she said almost primly. Then she swallowed hard. "My papa is one of them now. An inmate."

"This gent had the look of a hard case about him, not somebody who got locked up because his horse had thrown a shoe. I think the Institute is being used for far more than taking care of the crazy."

"I told you that my papa is not crazy. Uwe has paid money to them to keep Papa locked up so he can steal the ranch. Perhaps others in there are similarly imprisoned."

"Or not imprisoned at all," Slocum said, an idea coming to him. Laramie and the others' tracks had led directly to the Institute's front gate. They might be hiding there—and sampling Ludmilla's delights while the Rangers hunted the countryside. It sure beat most outlaw hideouts.

"What will you do?"

"You'd turn me in if I didn't go back and look for your pa," Slocum said.

"*Nein*, no, no, I would not. That was a bluff only. You are not an outlaw."

Slocum kept from laughing harshly. People saw what they wanted in others. Gretchen didn't want to think he was like Laramie, or even her brother, Uwe. So he wasn't.

Slocum knew he would not find it too difficult to throw down on Laramie and his partners and maybe even Uwe Helmann and put a couple slugs through them. He had long since learned not to let guilt over such shootings keep him awake at nights.

"I'll nose around now that I've scouted the place. There are armed guards everywhere, so getting in and out with your pa isn't going to be too easy."

"A bribe," Gretchen said suddenly. "You should bribe them. They are bad men and will be bought." She fished around in her shirt pocket directly over her left breast. Slocum wondered if she would let him look for whatever she sought. Then she pulled out a thin sheaf of greenbacks and handed them to him, thrusting out her arm straight and turning her face away slightly. She acted as if giving him the money was somehow painful.

"What's this for?"

"You will bribe these guards, if you need. If you do not, keep the money as pay for your help. You should not be blackmailed, as I did before. I am sorry that I said I would call for Ranger Coldcreek if you did not do what I said. But you are honest. You take the money, you bring me back my father."

Slocum tucked the money away. It looked to be a hundred dollars. He appreciated her trust in him not to take the money and leave. Gretchen couldn't know that he was after a considerable amount more. Wilson had cheated him out of eight hundred dollars, and Laramie had stolen a couple thousand. That was the kind of money he sought, not a young woman's pitiful few dollars.

"Eat more. Wrap what you do not finish and take as trail food," Gretchen said. "You can leave at first light."

"You surely are bossy, aren't you?"

Gretchen bristled.

"I know my own mind."

"Do you?" he asked softly. She sputtered as she sought some answer. "Never mind. I'll be back on the trail in an hour or so. I want to get back to the Breiland Institute just before dawn. That'll be the best time to sneak in over the wall."

"You will sneak in?"

"You wouldn't have wire cutters, would you?"

"I was fixing fence," Gretchen said. She went to her gear and bent over. Slocum caught his breath. There was a worldliness about Ludmilla that appealed to him, but the sheer innocence Gretchen showed, how unaware she was of the effect she had on him, made her all the more attractive.

And she was one pretty woman to start with.

"Here," she said. "I do not need them. Why do you take wire cutters?"

"The fence around the Institute has a couple strands on top. Cutting through will help me get in and out. I don't know what condition your pa will be in, and the only thing I know for sure, the front gate's not going to be how we get away." He pictured the four or five guards, in the tower and on the ground, and how they could train their powerful Sharps rifles on that gate. Anyone trying to escape the grounds that way would be blown into small, bloody chunks.

Slocum stowed what food he could in his saddlebags and sipped at the coffee. There was an uncomfortable silence between him and Gretchen. Every time he started to speak, he thought better of it. She was on edge and as jumpy as a flea on a hot griddle. Every sound in the dark startled her. The way her hand went to the six-shooter at her side told Slocum to let her be.

In less time than he had expected, he got to his feet and saddled his horse.

"You are going already?" He couldn't tell from her tone if she wanted him to clear out or she wanted him to stay.

"I can get to the Institute before dawn and sneak in. I thought it might be better to try getting in and out before dawn. This time of night the guards are starting to get bored and their attention drifts. I have to make as good a use of that as possible."

"I understand," Gretchen said. The blonde sounded sad.

Slocum took a gamble, went to her, planted a quick kiss on her slightly parted lips, then stepped back to see if she was going for her six-gun. Gretchen stood there staring up at him.

"I'll be back in two shakes of a lamb's tail," he said, swinging into the saddle. She lifted her hand in a half wave, then dropped it. She never said a word as he rode away. He wondered if he had shocked her or offended her—or had given her what she wanted. He laughed. Maybe he hadn't given her enough of what she wanted. There would be time when he got back with her pa to find out the details of what went on in her lovely blond head.

He rode steadily and reached the road sooner than expected. He also had the distinct feeling he was not alone on the road. Slocum pulled back on the reins and looked ahead at the thick undergrowth on both sides of the road. Trees sprouted up nearby and could conceal an ambush.

Or a posse.

He had developed patience as a sniper during the war, sometimes sitting all day for a single shot. Using some of that patience now flushed two men on the left side of the road. They came out with six-shooters blazing.

The lead tore through the air above his head. He bent low, worked to keep his horse under control, then put his heels to the animal's flanks and charged straight at the two gunmen. His unexpected move took them by surprise. They yelped and jumped back. One fell butt-first into a thorny bush. The other kept firing, but the shots went increasingly wild.

What Slocum did get out of the ambush, though, was one of them shouting for the Texas Ranger.

He had avoided the posse's trap. As he galloped along toward the Institute, he came to a quick decision. Coldcreek had not bought Gretchen's story that he worked for the Circle H. Everything about the Ranger's attitude had confirmed that. If he was caught by the posse, Slocum knew he would be taken back to Austin where Wilson would identify him as one of the robbers, no matter that the bank president hadn't seen him. By stringing him up, Wilson would eliminate an embarrassing and potentially dangerous threat to his reputation. Nobody was likely to believe Slocum when he said the banker had bilked him out of eight hundred dollars, but this eliminated any seed of doubt.

"After him!" came the cry from back along the road. Slocum recognized the Ranger's voice. That meant the entire posse was going to be after him.

Any chance for getting into the Institute unseen vanished. As he rode, a new plan came to Slocum. He had some ideas about what really went on at the Breiland Institute for the Insane, and this might be the best way of testing them out.

He galloped until his horse began to falter, but the Institute gates were ahead and open in welcome. He rode through and reined in, sending up a thick cloud of dust.

Gold Tooth came out, rifle ready.

Slocum didn't give him time to ask any questions.

"You gotta hide me," Slocum shouted. "The posse, a Ranger, after me!"

"I thought you would return," Dr. Poston said from the doorway. "Do come in. You will be safe here. For a price."

6

"Do come in," Dr. Poston said, bowing slightly. The smile on his face chilled Slocum to the bone. He felt like he was being invited into the spiderweb by a very hungry spider. The threat of the posse charging along behind him lent speed to his boots as he skidded across the floor just behind the two tall oak doors.

Poston closed the doors with a loud bang and silently pointed toward his office. Slocum was leery about letting the man walk behind him, but still went into the office and found a chair to sink into where he could watch both the door and Poston.

"You are a cautious man," Dr. Poston said. "I think you have chosen well coming here again."

"I didn't have any choice," Slocum said. "The posse's after me. A Texas Ranger is leading them."

Poston's thin eyebrow arched slightly. He sat and studied Slocum for a moment before responding.

"This is not what I expected. A Ranger after you?"

"The posse set an ambush along the road, but they got buck fever."

"Something that would never happen to you," Poston

said, more as an observation than a question. "You have done something very naughty, haven't you?"

"You looking to turn me in for a reward?"

Poston laughed. Slocum thought of a nail being dragged across plate glass.

"That is the farthest thing from my mind. In fact, the services offered by the Institute are far more extensive than the one you sampled previously. Oh, no, we don't allow any of our 'inmates' to be turned over to the law."

"Inmates?"

"Why, of course, you haven't seen the full menu of services available. More than those Ludmilla offers, there is the, hmm, call it sanctuary. We guarantee that lawmen never bother you within these walls."

"What's the catch?"

"There is no catch. There is only a fee for such a valuable service." Poston's eyes gleamed like a feral cat at the mention of money. "Fifty dollars a day. Some of our special inmates find it necessary to remain for some time before venturing into the world again. Life can be so cruel."

"It's even crueler with a noose around your neck," Slocum said. He fished in his pocket and found some of the money Gretchen had given him. "Here's for a couple days." He tossed the greenbacks onto Poston's desk. The director of the Institute made no move to take the money.

"Very good. This will be adequate for your stay until tomorrow midnight."

"Wait a minute," Slocum said, sitting straighter in the chair. "That's cheating me out of six hours or more."

Poston shrugged. The smile on his face told Slocum the director was sorry it wasn't later in the day.

"You've got a deal," Slocum said, not having to feign anger.

"Of course we do," Poston said. "You'll be given three squares and one visit a day from any of Ludmilla's ladies. There is no reason you cannot find this refuge pleasurable.

This is only one reason many of our inmates choose to stay longer."

A sudden rap at the office door caused Poston to reach for a drawer. Slocum figured he must have a six-shooter hidden there.

"What is it?" Poston snapped.

Gold Tooth shoved his head in and said, "The law, Boss. There's a real pushy Ranger who claims he tracked somebody right into the Institute. He won't go away and has a dozen men with him. None of them boys is lookin' too peaceable, either."

"We must allow the Ranger to poke about all he wants," Poston said. He held out his hand to keep Slocum from throwing down on him. "Do not fret, sir. We have our ways of keeping your presence here secret from even the most persistent of lawmen."

Poston swung about in his desk chair and tugged on a bell rope.

"Go with Jonah. Do exactly as he says and all will be well. And leave your side arm here."

Slocum saw a burly man half again his weight and topping his six feet by an easy four inches appear in a doorway leading to an adjoining room. Jonah stood with his loglike arms crossed on his chest. Tiny pig eyes stared at Slocum like he was dirt. Even with a six-shooter, Slocum was hardly a match for Jonah.

He unbuckled his gun belt and dropped it on Poston's desk. As Slocum was herded from the office, he caught sight of Poston putting the Colt Navy into a lower desk drawer.

"Where are we going?" Slocum asked Jonah as the huge man pushed him along with bumps from a belly that might have been carved from solid oak.

"Ahead," Jonah said.

"A man of few words," Slocum said. He let Jonah push him along, but he kept an eye peeled as they left the offices and exited into a hallway lined with iron doors. Slocum caught a glimpse of men in the cells, sitting and staring at nothing he could tell. Some were more violent and thrashed about in straightjackets. When they came to an empty cell, Jonah pointed inside.

"What should I do?"

"Act crazy," Jonah said. "Keep your face away from the door if anybody looks through the grille." Jonah tapped the short, strong bars over a hole cut in the metal door.

"This'll work?"

Jonah shrugged, shoved Slocum inside, and slammed the cell door behind with a ring of finality. Slocum was in here for the rest of his life if Poston chose to keep him here. He ran his hands over the cold iron of the door, and knew it would take a couple sticks of dynamite to blow it off the hinges. He pressed his ear against the metal and listened to the moans, shrieks, and other sounds that were the norm for this wing of the Institute. Slocum couldn't keep from shivering and it wasn't from cold.

Everyone locked up here was as crazy as a bedbug. Or were they? Slocum looked at his clothes and knew he would be in big trouble if the Ranger poked his ugly face against the grille. Even following Jonah's instructions about keeping his face turned wouldn't work. Ranger Coldcreek was no one's fool. He would remember what clothing Slocum had worn.

Working fast, Slocum stripped off his shirt and tossed it against the corridor wall. He heard an argument erupt outside. And his belly did a flip-flop when he recognized the Ranger's voice. Working frantically now, Slocum kicked off his boots and peeled his pants down around his ankles. He turned and bent over, presenting his backside to the door just as he heard scraping against the outside. Somebody was looking in, and Slocum hardly had to guess that it was Coldcreek.

"Jesus, you weren't jokin' when you said they're all loonies here," the Ranger said. Slocum heard spurs jingling as the Ranger moved along. He wanted to pull up his pants, but something told him to remain in this position, as embarrassing as it was. Slocum was glad he did.

A few seconds later, he heard movement just outside the cell door.

"Damnation, I can't hardly believe my eyes," Coldcreek said, and then came the sound of boots moving away echoed down the corridor. Only then did Slocum relax, pull up his pants, and get back into his boots and shirt. He laid his hand over the shirt pocket and the reassuring wad of greenbacks he had there.

Slocum wondered if Poston was an honest crook and stayed bought or if the lure of money was such that he let his inmates die in their cells and robbed them. The law would never know—or care.

Going back to the door, Slocum pressed his cheek against the door and tried to peer through the grate. All he saw was a section of wall in one direction and another locked cell door in the other. He backed away and examined the door more carefully, just in case he needed to escape. With enough time and the knife still tucked into the top of his boot, Slocum thought he could worry away enough mortar in the wall to cause the hinges to come free. It wouldn't take more than a few strong kicks to open the door that way since he didn't see that any of the cell doors were barred on the outside. Poston trusted the simple key locks.

Slocum flopped in the corner of the cell and waited. The cold from the stone floor and wall began to cause his bones to ache, but there wasn't any furniture in the room. All he had was a simple hole at the rear of the cell to take the place of a trip to the outhouse. The rising stench was overpowering, but Slocum kept telling himself gagging on the odor was better than choking with a noose around his neck.

He wasn't sure how long he was in the cell because he began to doze off. It had been too long since he'd gotten a good hour's sleep, much less an entire night's. The grating of a key in the lock woke him. His hand went to the hilt of his knife.

Jonah came in, the expression on his baby face unchanged. Slocum wondered if the man ever smiled or frowned or showed any emotion at all.

"Come on, Dr. Poston wants you," Jonah said.

"You can talk," Slocum said, climbing to his feet. Jonah only grunted in response.

They returned to Poston's office. The director of the Institute sat in his chair, making it look more like a throne.

"You were a very bad boy," Poston said. "The Ranger is very insistent on finding you. I am afraid you did a poor job hiding your trail since it definitely led straight here."

"Sorry," Slocum said insincerely. "I was rushed."

"That is all right. I employed one of my more inventive excuses. Is it not possible you are a master trailsman and laid a fake trail here? The Ranger found this dubious, but what other choice did he have but to believe it?"

Slocum laughed. Poston was an accomplished liar.

"I congratulate you, also, on your, hmm, impersonation of a lunatic. It impressed the Ranger more than anything else."

"How long before the posse's moved on?" Slocum asked.

"Oh, please, don't be in a hurry to leave. We are gracious hosts. I haven't told Ludmilla you are here once more, this time as a valued inmate, but she will be pleased. She took quite a shine to you. She never said, of course, but I could tell from her, hmm, special glow."

"I could use some food," Slocum said. His belly was growling with hunger.

"Of course. It is well past supper time, but the cook will find something for you. Jonah will show you the way."

"Is he going to follow me everywhere?"

"Oh, no, sir, he will lead you everywhere. This will ensure you don't get into trouble." Poston spoke coldly now, all business, no nonsense.

Slocum let Jonah hurry him from the office. This time they entered the lobby, giving Slocum a chance to look up the stairs. He didn't see any of Ludmilla's ladies of the

evening, but heard girlish giggles and low moans of pleasure coming from the third floor. Jonah bumped and
shoved him down the adjoining wing to a large room set
like an Army mess hall.

"I'll get you food," Jonah said.

Slocum sank down at the end of one table so he could
keep his eye on the door, as well as the kitchen where Jonah
worked to spoon out stew onto a tin plate. A slice of bread
and a cup of water finished the meal. Slocum looked at it on
the table in front and dived in. The stew wasn't particularly
good and the bread was moldy, but it might as well have
been a fine dinner served at San Francisco's Palace Hotel.

As he ate, Slocum watched Jonah closely. The man
seemed as impervious to emotion as any mountain peak,
but when a ruckus broke out in the hallway, Jonah moved
with more speed than Slocum had given him credit for. He
was not an opponent to underestimate.

Slocum finished his stew and went to the doorway. He
saw the huge man fighting with a man half his size dressed
in gray canvas. Slocum watched in surprise as Jonah struggled to hang on. Two other guards came and the three of
them subdued the inmate. As the man was swung around
before they threw him facedown to the floor, Slocum got a
shock of recognition.

The man looked exactly like Gretchen Helmann had described her father. Slocum knew better than to step out into
the hallway and draw Jonah's attention. He let the three
guards bodily pick up and carry off the man he thought
was Peter Helmann before following. They took Helmann
to another hallway. The cell doors in this wing all had locking bars rather the key locks in the other corridor. Slocum
peered around the corner and counted the doors down the
hall where they took him.

"Slocum!"

The unexpected use of his name caused Slocum to whirl
about and stare Carbuncle right in the eye. It was a toss-up
which man was more surprised.

"How'd you—" Carbuncle wasn't the quickest thinker in the world, but he knew Slocum shouldn't be inside the Breiland Institute for the Insane. The outlaw went for his pocket and had a derringer half pulled out when Slocum reacted. He bent, grabbed the handle of his knife, and swept up in a smooth motion that ended with the blade buried deep in Carbuncle's chest. Slocum felt the tip of the blade bounce off a rib and then slice through the man's heart. Carbuncle looked down at the blade sticking out of his chest, then up at Slocum.

"No," he said in a curiously ordinary voice, and then he died. His derringer fell from lifeless fingers to clatter to the floor. Slocum scooped it up, and turned back to see Jonah coming from the cell where he had carried Peter Helmann.

Reaching down, Slocum grabbed Carbuncle's collar and dragged the man along the hall, looking for a room with an unlocked door. He found one, dumped the body, and stepped out. His mind raced. He had no idea how long it would be until Carbuncle was discovered and an alarm raised. Dr. Poston was no fool. He would quickly go through the list of possible killers and Slocum would end up at the top, being the newest "inmate."

All he needed was to have Kinsley or Laramie spot him and the game would be over. He fingered the derringer and considered whether the two bullets loaded in it could bring down Jonah. He was getting around to believing it was possible when the pair of guards who had helped Jonah left Helmann's cell, barred the door, and hastened to join the big guard.

Slocum knew that attack was always a possibility, but sometimes retreat was more prudent. He waited in the cell for Jonah and the other guards to pass; then he slipped out. It would be only a matter of minutes before Jonah found that he was gone from the mess hall. Slocum doubted Jonah would raise a hue and cry immediately. He would hunt for Slocum, thinking he had wandered off after finishing his meal. But sooner or later, he would have to tell Dr. Poston that their reluctant guest had disappeared.

Slocum took a deep breath, then made his way back toward Poston's office. Clutching the derringer, Slocum swung into the office, ready to shoot the Institute director. The room was empty.

Slocum crossed the room and went around the desk. Poston had put Slocum's holster and six-shooter into a lower drawer. The first Slocum opened held only papers. The lower one was locked. Slocum put the derringer on the edge of the desk, and had bent to use his knife on the drawer when he heard footsteps approaching from the corridor he had just used.

Slocum dropped to his knees and hid behind the desk as Poston came in. Slocum clutched the knife, then realized he had left the derringer in plain sight on the desktop. Rather than reach for it and draw Poston's attention, he waited to see what would happen.

"Doctor!"

"What it is, Jonah?"

"The new inmate, the one you tole me to watch. He vanished."

Slocum wished he could see the expression on Poston's face, but the anger in his voice told the story well enough.

"Find him. Have you looked for him, you fool?"

Slocum would never have called that mountain of muscle and mean a fool, but Poston had the whip hand when it came to running the Institute.

"Yes, sir. All over the lower level."

"What about upstairs? What did Ludmilla say? Has she seen him?"

"Didn't go," Jonah said. "You tole me not to leave the ground floor."

Dr. Poston cursed, and Slocum heard the office door click shut. He hoped that Poston was on the other side as he chanced a quick peek around the corner of the desk. He heaved a sigh of relief. Poston had gone upstairs to ask Ludmilla if she had seen him.

Slocum grabbed the derringer and tucked it into his coat pocket, then used the knife to pry open the drawer with his six-shooter in it. The lock broke under his continued probing. It took only seconds for him to strap on his cross-draw holster and check the Colt Navy to be sure Poston had not tampered with the loads already in the cylinder.

Satisfied, he tucked the gun into the holster, stood, and started for the door. Then he stopped, spun Poston's chair around, and dropped heavily into it. He had to think. Simply going out the front door wasn't going to get him anywhere but dropped into a grave on the Institute grounds. This place was an armed camp. He needed a workable escape plan before he ventured out.

Slocum sat in the chair and his mind tumbled endlessly, nothing coming to him. He was inside a huge prison and couldn't see any easy way to get out now that Carbuncle was dead.

7

Slocum considered what he could do. Sitting in Poston's chair, waiting for the director to return and then holding him at gunpoint, was one way out, but Slocum increasingly disliked the notion. If half the men shouting and running around outside the office door were armed, one of them might take it into his head to be a marksman. Worse, either Laramie or Kinsley wouldn't care if they shot Poston.

Slocum got to his feet and looked out into the entryway. Since he was already inside the Institute, he might as well try to talk with Peter Helmann. If he freed the man, Helmann might even know a way out. Slocum didn't count on that being much of a chance, but Helmann had been locked up for a spell and had to know something about the guards and gates.

He had to wait several minutes before the search left the ground floor and went to the second. Slocum had no idea what was up there, but from his quick look on his way to the third floor whorehouse, it might be quarters for Poston, Ludmilla, and selected others, probably all soiled doves from the uppermost floor.

He sucked in a breath, let it out slowly, and stepped out. Empty. With long strides, Slocum went into the entryway and then down the far corridor where he had seen Jonah and the other two guards stuff Helmann into a cell. At least Slocum thought it was Peter Helmann. From Gretchen's description he had expected a younger man, but being locked up in the Institute might age a fellow. Slocum couldn't get the image of the guards working over the man from his head. Knotted ropes stung like hell when they hit bare flesh, and they had soaked those knotted ropes in water. Slocum didn't have to make too much of a leap of faith to believe it had been saltwater.

A quick look assured him no guards were in sight. Slocum pressed his eye to the grillwork and peered inside. A man huddled in the corner, arms wrapped around himself.

"Helmann?" Slocum called. "Are you Peter Helmann?" The man looked up. The side of his face looked like a side of beef. He had been methodically beaten. "Gretchen sent me to get you out."

"Gretchen?"

"Your daughter. You *are* Helmann, aren't you?"

"I want to . . ." The man's voice trailed off. He turned and spit blood. "I want out of here!" he said after clearing his mouth.

"Where're the keys to the cell doors?" Slocum had an idea of opening them all, letting the inmates roam free, and using the diversion to get the hell out of here, but these were well-secured doors. The locking bars were chained into place and then fastened with padlocks.

"Only one guard has them. Jonah. And he doesn't carry them all the time. Gets them from Poston." Helmann spit again. This time it was in anger, not from any need to get the blood from his mouth.

"Does the doctor keep the keys in his office?" Slocum looked back down the long gray hall and dreaded the prospect of returning to Poston's office. By now the guards would have finished searching the second floor. Ludmilla would know right away if anyone who didn't belong was on the third.

"On him, I think," Helmann gasped out. "Can't hardly breathe. Chest feels like I got ants gnawing at my lungs."

Slocum stepped back and examined the door. Knocking off the hinges would be impossible without a chisel and hammer. The lock on the chains was simple but sturdy. He had tried shooting off more than one lock in his day, and had always found it easier to chew away at the wood around it than to blast lead through it.

"I hear guards coming," Slocum said. "Don't give up. I'll be back for you."

"Get help. You can get out through the tunnels."

"Tunnels? What tunnels?" Slocum pressed flat against the wall when he saw a flash of white at the far end of the corridor. Someone in another cell began screeching like a hoot owl and this set off others. Slocum knew Jonah would come to quiet them, if only to see what had set off the racket. Edging along the wall to the far end of the corridor, he found a small alcove with a writing desk. A guard probably sat there during more normal times.

Slocum heard the steady click-click of boots hitting the stone floor as Jonah made his way down the corridor. Slocum wrapped his fingers around the butt of his Colt and waited. The first glimpse of Jonah he got, he would fire. The mountain of a man might take several slugs to bring down. Slocum had slid the six-shooter partly from the holster when he heard the steps only yards off. Then came a shuffling sound and receding footfalls. He chanced a quick look around, and saw Jonah's broad back vanishing toward Dr. Poston's office. The director must have called all his staff together to organize a new search.

Slocum felt trapped at the end of the corridor until he saw a trapdoor under the writing desk. He pushed the desk to the side, partly exposing it. If Jonah noticed, Slocum was in hot water. But a tug on the iron ring mounted in the trapdoor revealed a gaping darkness below. Dropping to his knees, Slocum saw a rickety ladder. He swung over the edge, got his feet onto the ladder, and pulled the trapdoor shut above him. For an instant he hung in complete darkness; then his eyes adjusted and he saw faint light seeping into the tunnel below.

He went down the ladder, and almost fell when one rung broke. Slocum caught himself, paused, and listened hard for any sign his accident had alerted the guards. He dropped the rest of the way to the gravel floor in the tunnel. Fumbling about, Slocum pulled out the tin of lucifers and lit one, holding the sputtering match high over his head. The light showed a long narrow tunnel leading back under the Institute. Slocum thought this might be part of an escape system Poston had built in case of danger.

The inmates might get free, the "inmates" who paid for sanctuary might get rowdy and decide to recover the money Poston extorted, or more likely, Poston wanted a way out if the law ever came after him.

Slocum walked quickly down the tunnel, pausing when he reached a junction. Just as the match flared and burned out, Slocum caught his breath. He stepped to the side and felt the cold stone wall against his arm, drew his six-gun, and lit another lucifer.

"Son of a bitch," Slocum muttered. He holstered his six-shooter and went closer to a niche in the tunnel. The remains of a man hung there, held by iron shackles. Moving along the tunnel, Slocum found four more corpses, hardly skeletons, showing that the men had died over a span of months, if not years. Slocum wondered if Helmann had been shackled here so he could see the dead bodies in an effort to coerce him to do what Poston wanted—whatever that might be.

Slocum cursed again as the match burned his fingers. He stood amid the chained death and let his eyes adapt again to the utter darkness. As before, he saw a small glimmer of light. This time he made his way toward it, carefully placing his feet to be sure he didn't step into a hole. He stopped and looked up at a bright rectangle of light seeping around another trapdoor. Carefully mounting the ladder, he got his shoulder against the wooden door and lifted slightly. The sudden light dazzled him, but he didn't move. He heard men in the room.

"You don't know his name?" Laramie pounded his fist on Poston's desk. "He killed Carbuncle! He killed my partner and you don't know who you let into this goddamn place?"

"The Ranger and his posse were hot on his heels," Dr. Poston said uneasily. "I had seen him here before, and there was no trouble."

"You let him kill Carbuncle," Laramie said.

"We do not know that is what happened," Poston said. "One of the other inmates might be responsible."

"A knife to the gut?"

"What can I say?" Poston spread his hands and tried to look innocent. From where Slocum spied on the men, Poston didn't do too good a job.

"I want Carbuncle's money back. All of it."

Poston sputtered, then nodded and said, "Very well. That seems fair. Would you like me to divide it between you and Mr. Kinsley?"

Laramie jerked as if Poston had struck him with a whip. The director was pointing out that he still held some control over the matter.

"Apply it to our stay. Both of us," Laramie said. "We might have to stay here a while longer, thanks to you lettin' the posse sniff around."

"We will work out something equitable," Poston said. He had regained some measure of his confidence. "Might I recommend you and your friend go upstairs and allow Madam Ludmilla to find you suitable ways of passing the time while my staff hunts the intruder?"

Laramie spit out something too low for Slocum to overhear, spun, and for a moment faced Slocum. Then he walked out without noticing the small crack between trapdoor and the floor. Slocum twisted around and saw Poston sit heavily behind his desk. From the sour expression, Poston had noticed Slocum had jimmied open the drawer and now knew he faced an armed adversary.

Poston rocked back in his chair, thought for a moment, then bellowed, "Jonah! Get in here. Immediately!"

Slocum lowered the door slightly as the hulking guard entered.

"We do another check of the ground floor. Be certain to look in the tunnels, also. And put someone with a rifle at the landing on the second floor to guard Ludmilla and her girls in their rooms."

"Nobody out of their rooms on the second floor?" asked Jonah.

"No one. And if we still don't find him, we search everyone's room. And I mean everyone's."

"Yes, sir," Jonah said. Slocum saw the first hint of emotion on the man's face. He smiled at the idea of having to search the prostitutes' rooms.

Jonah left, and Poston followed almost immediately. Slocum pushed up the trapdoor and saw that a throw rug had been glued to the top to keep anyone from finding it by accident. He quickly went to the director's desk and began rummaging through the drawers. What he searched for, he couldn't say. Keys? More likely, Poston had them with him now. Slocum mostly wanted something to show what was going on here. If he could find records showing that Poston imprisoned men like Peter Helmann knowing they were sane, Gretchen might be able to take the evidence to the Texas Ranger and close this place down.

Slocum smiled grimly. Who knows how many outlaws would be flushed from the brothel upstairs?

He gave up when he found nothing useful. Going to a file cabinet and pawing through the folders there yielded nothing he could use, either. What he needed as much as anything else was a map of the entire Institute. He had caught a glimpse from Ludmilla's room on the third floor in the turret. With a little luck he might be able to map the entire place and figure out a quick way of escaping—with Peter Helmann.

Slocum went to the door, saw no one in the lobby, and made his way cautiously up the steps to the second floor. Poston had ordered a guard here, but Slocum couldn't see him. The hallways were lined with doors. The guard and one of the girls might be enjoying a little dalliance. If so, Slocum hoped it was a long dalliance. He hurried on up the stairs to the third floor, then took the steps up the spiral staircase to Ludmilla's aerie two at a time.

The etched-glass windows let in early morning light from all directions. Slocum went to one window and examined it. Using his knife blade, he pried it loose and pulled the pane down and set it on the floor, giving an unobstructed view of the Breiland Institute for the Insane. He saw that there were wings he had not even realized existed. To keep up appearances, Poston might actually keep lunatics here. Hiding outlaws among them would be easy enough, as long as he didn't get confused and let out the wrong inmate.

Slocum doubted that would ever happen. Poston knew where his money came from. He might get some small change from the state for keeping the insane, but his real money came from prostitution and the tariff received for hiding outlaws on the run.

Slocum spent another ten minutes being certain he had the layout firmly in mind. He had no idea how he was going to get Peter Helmann free, and he might not be able to without adequate help. Nobody on Poston's staff knew he was looking to spring Helmann. That kept the man safe— or as safe as he was at the moment. If Poston caught wind of Slocum trying to get Helmann free, there would be yet another corpse dangling from chains in the tunnels below the Institute.

The window would give away that he had been here, but Slocum didn't care. Let them go hunting across the sloping roofs for him. He gave one quick look at the fifteen-foot drop and knew that wasn't a sensible escape route. The sniper in the far turret would be able to pick him off easily.

Slocum hurried down the spiral staircase to the third floor and across the parlor to the stairs leading to the second floor. He froze when he saw Kinsley at the landing. The outlaw was arguing with someone and didn't see Slocum, but Slocum had nowhere to hide. If he moved, this would draw attention. Holding his position became harder by the second; then Kinsley went back down to the second floor, abandoning the landing.

On cat's feet Slocum went back up to the third floor. Dropping to the roof from the turret hadn't been a good idea, and escaping across the roof was dangerous. But it had just become impossible to get away inside the building with Kinsley below him on the staircase. One glance and Kinsley would know who the man raising the ruckus was and would open fire.

Slocum went to a window and pried it open. The steeply sloping shingled roof afforded no footing at all, but he had no choice. He got his leg over the sash and gingerly tapped about with his boot for purchase.

"Stop!"

Slocum saw Kinsley coming up the stairs, whipped out his six-shooter, and fired at the outlaw. Kinsley tried to draw and dodge the bullet at the same instant. All he succeeded in doing was losing his balance and falling backward down the stairs.

Slocum had no time to crow about Kinsley's fate because he shifted his own weight and his foot skidded out from under him. He grabbed for the window frame and lost his balance, hitting the roof belly-down and sliding toward the edge of the roof. At the last possible instant he felt his feet hit a rain gutter. The tin gutter came loose with a loud crash and fell two stories, hitting the ground with a noise so loud it could awaken the dead.

Feet kicking, fingers slowly slipping, Slocum clung to

the edge of the roof. He had announced his location with the clatter. Now he presented himself as a perfect target to the marksman in the far turret. He waited for the bullet that would explode in his spine.

8

Slocum kicked frantically trying to get a foothold. He couldn't swing far enough under the eaves to find anywhere along the wall. Slowly, strength fading in his hands, he knew he had no choice. He braced himself, then let loose and fell. He hit the ground hard, let his knees sag under him, and rolled to the side. He smashed up hard enough against the house to make it sound like a drumbeat. Stunned, Slocum slowly shook off the effect of the two-story drop. It had been hard, but would have been worse if he had come down from the third floor. The slide against the pitched roof had not seemed like a desirable thing at the time, but it got him to the second-floor roof and a fall he'd managed to survive.

Getting to his feet, he was a little shaky as he stumbled along. He looked up into the tower for sign of the rifleman there. Empty. But then the bell began ringing. Guards swarmed from the front of the main building, all waving their rifles around. The bell warned of an inmate escaping.

Slocum touched the ebony handle of his six-shooter. He was no mere inmate. He could shoot back. Pressing himself against the wall, he edged away from the front, got to the side, and then ran hell-bent for leather toward the distant stables. Every second he expected to be seen and cut down. Panting harshly, he reached the barn and burst inside.

A stableman looked up, startled. Slocum drew, cocked, and aimed his six-gun directly at the man's face.

"My horse. Saddle it," Slocum said.

"Whatever you say, mister," the man said. He had turned as pale as a bleached muslin sheet at the sight of the gun pointed in his direction. As the stableman gathered Slocum's gear and got it on his horse, Slocum looked around. Fifteen horses.

He motioned for the man to get to the rear of the barn. The instant the man neared a door in the side, he ducked through it, screaming for help at the top of his lungs. Slocum didn't care. If anything, it helped him get away. He shooed the other horses from their stalls, mounted his own horse, and started a stampede out the main doors toward the front gate.

Before, he had been lucky in avoiding the guards. Now every one aimed their rifle at him. Slocum kept low, hooted and hollered, and kept himself in the middle of the herd thundering toward the gate. The guards brought down several of the frightened horses, but Slocum finally burst through the gates and galloped away. Bullets sang above him. After what seemed an eternity, he was out of range.

He let out a whoop of glee. He was unhurt and had escaped. Even better, Laramie and Kinsley and any of the guards wouldn't be able to follow until they ran down their horses. As frightened as those horses had been with bullets zinging all around them, they might not stop running until they reached Brownsville.

Then his cheerfulness faded. Peter Helmann was still in the Institute. And the Ranger and the posse still hunted for him. Now he had added new enemies out to put a bullet in his skull. Slocum wondered if Kinsley had gotten a good look at him, or if it mattered. Laramie had suspected who Carbuncle's killer was. The only thing that might keep

Laramie and Kinsley off his trail was the threat of the Texas Ranger.

And there was a big problem with that. The Ranger was just as likely to want to throw him in jail as Laramie was to kill him.

Slocum fumbled around and found the map Gretchen had given him. He tried to figure out where the main ranch house for the Circle H was. He had no way of reaching her other than going to the ranch. From what she had said about her brother, this might not be too smart on Slocum's part, but he needed help if he was to get her father out. The brief exchange he'd had with Peter Helmann convinced him that the man was not locked up in the lunatic asylum because he was crazy. The man had been lucid, but tortured to the breaking point.

How much longer Helmann could last was a question Slocum didn't want to explore. Get him out, then deal with the court order and crooked judge who had put him in the Breiland Institute for the Insane.

Slocum finally got an idea where the Circle H ranch house must be and cut off the road. He had gone less than a quarter mile when he heard the pounding of horses' hooves along the road. Sawing at his horse's reins, he trotted into a stand of maple trees and watched his back trail. He cursed under his breath. He would have bet every dime stolen in the bank robbery that Laramie and Kinsley lacked the sand to come after him. But both outlaws were pissed enough at him to leave the safety of the Institute in the hope of gunning him down. Slocum hadn't thought Carbuncle had meant that much to either of the men.

Unless there was some other reason they came riding bold as brass into the Hill Country.

Slocum drew his Winchester from its sheath and lifted it to his shoulder. He gauged the distance. It was a hundred yards, but for him it wasn't an impossible shot, even with the faint breeze blowing right to left. He could correct for that, but he didn't lever a round into the chamber. Even at this distance, the sound might alert the two robbers. But Slocum would fire if they found his tracks and came this direction.

A smile curled the corners of his lips when he saw the men arguing over which set of tracks to follow. Laramie prevailed. They rode away at an angle, heading more toward Mexico than in his direction. He wondered how long it would be until they figured out they had the wrong trail.

That hardly mattered. By the time they found his real trail, he would be at the Circle H talking with Gretchen.

Slocum hadn't ridden more than five minutes when he heard voices booming through the forest. He sat straighter in the saddle and listened hard.

". . . pay or I'm leavin'."

"You know there's no money to pay ya out here," came a familiar drawl. Slocum reached for his six-shooter although the Ranger was probably still some distance away. From the sound of horses, he was with his posse.

"You gotta pay up, Ranger. We cain't go on fer ever out here. We're ridin' in circles."

"That's because you keep losing the trail." Ranger Coldcreek's tone brooked no argument, but he got it anyway.

"I'm the best durn tracker in the Hill Country, and I say he rode into that there crazy farm. Might be they locked him up and you didn't look in the right cell."

"He wasn't there. Why would Dr. Poston lie?"

Slocum wondered at the Ranger's gullibility. The lawman hadn't looked into every cell. That would have taken a full day, so he'd relied on Poston's word.

"That man's a caution, ain't he?" said another posse member.

Slocum began easing his horse at an angle to the spot where the lawmen argued. As much as he wanted to hear what they were up to, he had to reach Gretchen and tell her about her father. If Coldcreek stopped him, Slocum might never get word to the woman.

"What's that mean?"

"Hell, Ranger, you know what I mean," said the posse member, laughing. "Ever'body here knows what I mean."

Slocum missed the discussion on the whorehouse on the third floor as he wound in and out of the trees and came to an open stretch of lush grass that would be perfect for grazing cattle. It was, he found out too late, also perfect for two outlaws who wanted to rest and let their horses sample the juicy grass.

Laramie looked up and saw him. He nudged Kinsley, who let out a shout as he went for his six-shooter. Kinsley was firing before he cleared leather. Slocum saw the man wince and grab his leg where he had shot himself in his hurry to plug Slocum. Laramie was more methodical. He drew his rifle from the saddle scabbard and began firing with deadly aim. Slocum jerked to the side as a bullet tore through his shirt sleeve. It missed his skin, but not by enough.

Laramie was something of a marksman and was getting the range.

Slocum ducked and prodded his horse to keep it moving. This made Laramie's job all the harder, but the man seemed up to it. Two more leaden hornets buzzed past Slocum's head. Laramie was shooting to kill.

Rather than gallop away, Slocum cut back and let the men see him again. Both had mounted and were charging toward him on tired horses. Slocum knew it was too much to hope that both horses would step into prairie-dog holes and break their legs. But this was almost as good. Laramie couldn't shoot accurately while he was riding.

As their horses visibly tired, Slocum swung around and retraced his path into the woods. He rode straight for the posse hidden among the trees. At first he thought he heard someone still arguing with the Ranger; then all sound disappeared.

Slocum knew they had heard him and the gunfire directed at him. He judged how far away from the posse he might be, then veered sharply and plunged down into a shallow ravine. He found the stream that cut it and went up the far bank into a thicket. Here he took another risk and jumped from his horse. He held its reins tightly and kept the horse from moving about.

Hearing was the only sense that served him now. Laramie and Kinsley galloping straight along the trail—into the open arms of the Texas Ranger and his posse.

The fusillade from the posse destroyed the relative silence in the forested area. Their slugs ripped through leaves and whined off rocks and crashed with dull *thuds* into tree trunks. Laramie and Kinsley returned fire, then understood the full depth of their trouble. Slocum smiled when he reckoned both outlaws we e out of ammo. He heard two horses retreating toward the meadow, and knew Laramie and Kinsley were in a race for their lives now.

The full posse tore after them. Although Slocum couldn't see it, he guessed Ranger Coldcreek was in the lead. In the dense underbrush, Slocum waited a full five minutes before getting back into the saddle. He would have to make a circle far out of his way getting to the Circle H ranch, but it would be worth it.

Especially if the Ranger nabbed both Laramie and Kinsley. He would have a pair of desperados for the bank robbery and might forget all about John Slocum. The posse would definitely want to return straightaway to Austin to collect their rewards. If this happened, Slocum felt that everything would be tied up all neat and proper with a big red ribbon.

9

Slocum reached the Circle H at sundown. He stopped at the wide gate leading into the yard in front of the ranch house and felt a shiver up and down his spine. Over the years he had come to rely on his sense of impending danger. It had kept him from being killed more times than he cared to count, and it was screaming at him now that this peaceful ranch house wasn't so peaceful.

He studied the house. It was modest for the size of the Circle H. A large barn some distance downhill where a stream ran, providing water for both men and animals, couldn't have looked more serene. In the corral were a half-dozen saddle horses, but none of them was Gretchen's. Hers might be in the barn. He wished he could take a gander at the horses already in their stalls, but a cowboy came from the bunkhouse, stopped, and looked hard at him.

"Cat's out of the bag," Slocum said softly to his horse, patting it on the neck. He was hungrier than he could remember, and the horse was sorely in need of hay or maybe a nose bag of grain.

"Howdy, mister," the cowboy said, coming over and pushing his floppy-brimmed hat back to get a better look at

Slocum. "You lose your way?"

"Just passing through," Slocum said. He wanted to ask after Gretchen, but this wasn't something that felt right. "Could I get some of that water running along downhill and maybe some fodder for my horse?"

"Don't see why not," the cowboy said, stroking his stubbled chin. "I'll hafta ask the ramrod, though. He's in charge of the whole danged spread right now."

"Getting ready to drive the cattle north?"

"That's what they say. Seems a little early in the season to me. Calves hardly wobble next to their mamas, but ain't up to me. Come on in. I'll scare up Billy. Don't see why you shouldn't get some chow, too, if you want."

"That's mighty neighborly," Slocum said. He dismounted and walked in silence to the ranch house.

"Be right back," the cowboy said. He had been genial enough to this point. Now he looked as if he had to bite off his own tongue and swallow it. Slocum decided the cowboy wasn't too keen on talking with the ramrod, for some reason.

The hand knocked on the door, waited, knocked again. A florid man standing hardly five-foot-five opened the door.

"Whatcha want?"

The cowboy spoke in a tone too low to overhear, but he pointed at Slocum several times. Slocum didn't have to hear the words to know the short man wasn't inclined to go along with any charitable giving.

"That's all right," Slocum called. "I'll mosey on."

"Wait, don't. go yet," the cowboy said. His attitude changed as he faced the one Slocum suspected to be Billy, the Circle H ramrod. The cowboy pointed a couple more times, and finally Billy backed down.

"Git on over to the bunkhouse and grab some chuck," Billy shouted. "You kin sleep in a spare bunk tonight, but come mornin', you're on your way."

"Thanks for the hospitality," Slocum said, not bothering

to keep the sarcasm out of his tone. The cowboy hurried back down the steps. Billy slammed the door.

"Don't go judgin' the rest of us by him. He and the owner's boy are thicker 'n thieves and don't always do what's right."

"Where's the boss?" Slocum asked. He wanted to hear the cowboy's answer.

"That's a right complicated subject," he said, shaking his head. "Family matter, I'd call it."

"So his son's in there?" Slocum jerked his thumb back toward the ranch house.

"Nope, he's out ridin' fence."

"Must be a good man to work for if he does a ranch hand's work like that and the ramrod's staying in the main house," said Slocum.

"Ain't like that. Not exactly. Wish Gretchen would run things."

"Daughter?" Slocum tried to keep the eagerness from his voice. He wanted to know where she had gotten off to.

"Yep, purty as a bug, too. She's in town right now."

"Austin? That's a day's hard ride off," Slocum said.

"Naw, there's a small town name of Knipsen not far from here. Not more 'n ten miles. She went in for supplies." The cowboy made it sound like he hoped that was where Gretchen had gone, but believed something worse had happened to her.

"Saw a passel of men riding across the countryside," Slocum said. "Is there a range war brewing?"

"Nothin' like that," the cowboy denied. "You kin take that bunk on the end," he said, holding open the bunkhouse door. "I'll see if Cookie can scare up some grub for you."

"Glad someone on the Circle H is so hospitable," Slocum said. The man grinned crookedly, then lit out to find the cook. He didn't see what Slocum had—Billy had come back out on the porch, straining to overhear their conversation. When Billy saw that Slocum had spotted him, the ramrod stepped back into deeper shadows, as if he could become totally invisible. Slocum shrugged off the eavesdropping.

He stowed his gear, then led his horse to the barn, fed, watered, and curried the animal. By the time he returned to the bunkhouse a tin plate of stew had been put on his bunk. He scooped it up and wolfed down the food. The Circle H cook was a damn sight better than the Institute cook working with the same raw materials.

When Slocum finished his meal, he cleaned off the plate the best he could, then put it aside. Nobody else was in the bunkhouse. Slocum poked his head outside and looked around. The ranch looked deserted except for the light burning in the window of the house. Even the cowboy who had argued with the ramrod to give Slocum food and a place to rest his head was nowhere to be seen. This was more than passing odd, but Slocum shrugged it off. Nothing about this ranch could be considered normal when the owner's son put his father into a lunatic asylum, the daughter was at odds with her brother over it, and the ramrod bunked down in the family's house and seemed to run things while the son was out riding fence.

Slocum didn't even want to know where the foreman was.

He returned to his bunk, flopped down, and stared up at the ceiling. A large crack showed him part of the night sky. He stared at the stars slowly appearing and disappearing behind clouds, and was soon asleep.

Slocum came awake with a start and jerked so hard he fell off the bed. It saved his life. An ax cut all the way through the thin mattress and embedded in the frame. Struggling to pull it free for another try at splitting Slocum's head open was the short ramrod. Billy cursed and kicked against the bed to get the ax free, then backed off and went for his six-shooter.

Slocum never gave him a chance. The derringer he had taken from Carbuncle belched fire once, twice. In the darkness his aim wasn't good, but he hit the ramrod at least once from the grunt, followed by even more fulmination.

Slocum shoved the two-shot pistol back into his pocket and grabbed for his Colt Navy, holstered and hung on the post at the head of the bed. He found himself wrestling with Billy over it. Somehow, the ramrod had decided not to fire on him with his own six-gun and tried to grab Slocum's.

Twisting hard, Slocum landed his elbow into the middle of the man's back. This drove Billy to the floor and gave Slocum the chance to draw his own six-shooter. He stepped back and aimed it at the ramrod, still gasping for breath.

"Why'd you try to kill me?" Slocum demanded. "I don't cotton much to back-shooters or fools and I think you're a little of both. You got three seconds to tell me why you tried to kill me."

Billy rolled over and sat up, clutching his side. The man's shirt was soaked with blood.

"You shot me. You shot me! I wasn't doin' nuthin' and you shot me."

"That ax just happened to miss my head," Slocum said, "and your fingers were wrapped around the handle." Slocum cocked his pistol.

"You got this all wrong, mister," Billy said.

Slocum didn't hear any movement behind him, but saw the suddenly furtive look in the ramrod's eyes. With a motion as abrupt as when he had thrown himself out of the bunk, Slocum jumped left and slammed hard into the bunkhouse wall. Again his quick reaction saved him. An ax handle whizzed through the air where his head had been a fraction of a second before. He swung and grappled with the man who had tried to bean him.

In an instant, Slocum found himself fighting both men. He squeezed off a round and heard Billy yelp as he winged the man again.

"He got, me, Boss, he got me good this time."

Slocum doubted that since Billy was still talking. But he tried to get a good look at the man he still fought. Billy had called him "Boss." Slocum thought this must be Uwe Helmann, but wanted to see his face. But before he could, he stumbled over Billy and sat down heavily on the bed. Before he could swing his Colt around and fire, both men hightailed it from the bunkhouse.

Grabbing his gear, Slocum went to the door and looked around the moonlit yard. The pair had vanished like rabbits down a hole. Slocum considered how easy it would be for them to ambush him. They knew the lay of the land here, and he didn't. Worse, they had already shown they had the grit to kill him without the courtesy of looking him square in the eye.

He cocked his head to one side and listened hard, but heard nothing but the uneasy stirring of the horses in the corral. Slocum had to cross an open stretch of yard to get to the barn. He ran a zigzag path until he got to the barn door, then slid into the darkness. Wasting no time, he saddled his horse and led it out. An itchy feeling ran up and down his spine as he imagined Billy or the man he had called Boss drawing a bead on him. Keeping low, Slocum rode from the Circle H, and heaved a sigh of relief when he got on the other side of the gate.

More than once Slocum had worn out his welcome, but seldom had it been this quick. He rode along the road and came to a fork. He judged where he had been and where the town the cowboy had mentioned might lie. If Gretchen was in Knipsen, he wanted to talk to her and get this straightened out. He had thought he might wait for her to return to the Circle H, but from the reception he had received, she might be greeted with even less bonhomie.

Moving slowly to conserve his horse's strength and to listen for the sounds of pursuit, Slocum rode along and wondered if all this woe was worth it. The more he thought about it, the angrier he got. Wilson had cheated him. Laramie and Kinsley had double-crossed him. The Ranger wanted his scalp. Billy and Gretchen's brother had tried to murder him. Those were all good reasons not to simply leave the Texas Hill Country.

An even better one was Peter Helmann. No man should be locked up like an animal the way Poston had imprisoned Helmann.

Slocum rode as long as he could, but when he started falling asleep in the saddle he knew he had to rest. His horse stumbled in the dark, and his own energy was coming to an end. Slocum found a spot well off the road to pitch his bedroll, put hobbles on his horse, and then stretched out. He was asleep within minutes, waking only when the morning sun filtered through the sweet-gum tree leaves.

The trip into Knipsen took the better part of three hours, and he reached the main street just short of noon. The town was like a hundred others he had seen. Ranching kept it alive. More than one feed store and general mercantile kept the money flowing through an otherwise dry riverbed. His nose wrinkled when the scent of a bakery working on another batch of bread reached him. Slocum dismounted, tethered his horse, and then froze on the steps leading into the bakery.

". . . a good addition," came a voice he remembered all too well. Dr. Poston stepped out of the general store next to the bakery. The man carried an armful of supplies.

Slocum turned his face away and headed for the side of the bakery, where he spun around and peered around the corner. Following Poston from the store were Ludmilla and Jonah.

"I am not liking this very much," Ludmilla said. "It can be wrong."

"Wrong? Not that. A lovely blonde like her will more than pay for her keep. You worry too much about morality, for a woman in your chosen profession, Ludmilla."

"Not so good, *nyet*," she said.

"Jonah, see to our new staff member." Dr. Poston pointed down the street.

The hulking guard nodded once and set off with a quick

pace that belied his size. Again, Slocum had to remind himself Jonah was both big and fast. Slocum would have followed, but had no way to get past Poston and Ludmilla without being seen. Then he decided that they wouldn't leave town without Jonah.

Poston dropped his armload into the wagon, then climbed into the driver's box. He let Ludmilla make her own way to the hard bench beside him. With more expertise than Slocum would have thought the man possessed, Poston got the team moving, swung about in a tight circle, and headed in the direction Jonah had gone.

There was no way he could lose them if they stayed with the wagon, and Slocum reckoned they would. He went into the bakery, bought himself a loaf of freshly baked bread for a nickle, and left, gnawing at a hunk ripped from the end. At the far end of town Slocum saw Jonah carrying out what looked like a rug. He dumped it into the rear of the wagon, hopped up, and sat beside it. Slocum couldn't be sure, but thought the bundle moved about on its own. The struggles stopped when Jonah reached over and pushed down hard. Then the wagon rattled out of town.

"Pardon me," Slocum said, stopping a man entering the bakery. "What's down the road in that direction?"

"Nuthin' you'd want," the man said. "If you're headin' to Austin, it's that way." He pointed down a road that headed at right angles to Knipsen's main street.

"But that way?"

"The Hill Country's answer to Bedlam, that's what's out there. You want a loony, you go there. You want Austin, you go the other road. Not a whale of a lot else out here that'd interest you."

Slocum was even more certain now what had been wrapped up in the roll Jonah had dumped into the wagon, and it caused his ire to rise again. He spent too much time being mad and not enough time doing anything about it.

Holding the rest of the bread in his teeth, he mounted and started riding out of town, following Poston and his cronies.

Slocum didn't have a doubt in the world they were heading for the Breiland Institute for the Insane and their "paying" package in the back was Gretchen Helmann.

10

Slocum finished his bread and his plan for getting Gretchen free at about the same time. From the speed of the wagon, Poston would never be able to reach the Institute before sundown. Slocum doubted the director was the kind to drive at night. A more chilling prospect had also occurred to Slocum—Poston might want to sample the unwilling new recruit to Ludmilla's stable.

Getting past Jonah would be the hard part, but Slocum touched the stock of his Winchester and knew, no matter how big the guard might be, enough lead in his belly would eventually stop him.

Other plans beyond getting Gretchen free from Poston flickered through his mind, too. If he succeeded in getting the drop on Poston, he might use the man as a hostage to free Peter Helmann. It seemed fair. Poston's life for Helmann's freedom. If Poston was actually in charge and there was no Breiland ordering him about, Slocum stood a good chance of getting the Helmanns free and even wresting the bank robbery money from Laramie.

After a long afternoon of travel, Poston pulled over to a spot where the grass had been cut up by other wagon wheels. Slocum guessed this might be a halfway point for

the doctor when traveling from the Institute to Knipsen. If
so, Poston felt safe here. That made it all the easier for
Slocum to get Gretchen away.

Jonah fixed an evening meal and Poston sat with Ludmilla, talking in low voices. Slocum slipped around and
came within ten yards of their camp, eyeing the roll of canvas in the rear of the wagon. He couldn't say for certain
what was trapped within, but it was about Gretchen's size.

"Get her," Poston barked.

Slocum slipped behind the bole of a tree and watched
Jonah come to the wagon and heave the roll out. He let it
fall on the ground and got a muffled cry of protest from inside. Jonah began unrolling the canvas and Gretchen eventually rolled free, too dizzy to stand. Jonah grabbed her,
pulled her to her feet, and steered her toward the campfire.

Seeing his chance, Slocum stepped out, six-shooter in
his hand, ready to buffalo Jonah. The man might have a
head made out of solid granite, but a steel barrel laid alongside his temple enough times was sure to bring him to his
knees. Once the guard was out of action, Slocum doubted
there would be any trouble getting the drop on Poston and
Ludmilla.

He moved quickly to the wagon, hopped into the bed,
and went to the far side, ready to swing and connect with
Jonah's head. Again, Slocum had misjudged how fast the
guard moved. Jonah was several paces away, roughly shoving Gretchen ahead of him. Slocum decided stealth wasn't
going to work. He aimed the six-gun, but held off when
Jonah grabbed Gretchen and swung her around, between
him and Slocum.

Slocum stood as still as a statue, thinking Jonah had
heard him. But the giant of a man was only wrestling with
an increasingly feisty Gretchen Helmann.

"Don't," Jonah said. "Don't try to get away, or I'll hurt
you."

"You son of a bitch!" Gretchen raged. She aimed a kick
at the man's groin. Jonah turned slightly and took her foot

on his thigh. He grunted with pain, but otherwise showed no sign that she'd bothered him at all. Jonah picked her up, kicking and cursing, and slung her over his shoulder. Slocum didn't dare fire now or he would hit Gretchen.

He jumped to the ground and followed Jonah to the campfire, staying just out of the circle of illumination from the guttering flames. Slocum pointed his six-shooter at Poston, then lowered it. There was no way he could hope to get the drop on the director while Jonah was wrestling with Gretchen. Seeing Poston draw a small pistol convinced him rescuing Gretchen using a frontal assault would only endanger her life. Slocum backed away quietly, still unseen, and returned to the wagon. He slipped under it and hunkered down near a wheel where he wouldn't be easily seen.

Slocum decided waiting them out was the only way to rescue Gretchen. But after several hours, he didn't get a chance to pluck her from Jonah's clutches. The guard sat beside her, and Poston watched with a hawkish eye. Only Ludmilla slept. Slocum never saw an opportunity to move in, especially after Jonah wrapped her in the canvas roll once more. Two quick shots might do the trick; Slocum wasn't above shooting the men in cold blood, if it would have accomplished anything. It didn't seem possible that he could take out Poston without Jonah responding. If he shot Jonah first, Poston would use his small pistol.

Giving up galled him, but there wasn't any way he could stop the men without endangering Gretchen. He slipped away into the night, figuring he would trail them in the morning and see if a chance opened for him.

It didn't. Slocum rode some distance off the road, watching carefully. Jonah and Poston had undoubtedly transported more violent, stronger inmates than Gretchen Helmann and knew how to deal with their struggles. Even swooping in, gun blazing away, didn't look like it would work. With growing frustration, Slocum watched the wagon vanish through the front of the Institute.

He swung around and trotted back in the direction of

Knipsen. Getting Gretchen out as soon as possible became his primary goal since she was in more danger than her father. He could pick a spot and shoot any man riding into the Breiland Institute from the saddle, figuring they were going to visit Ludmilla and her Cyprians—and Gretchen—but that would only give away his presence. Slocum's best advantage right now was Poston not knowing he had trouble prowling around just outside the walls.

Slocum returned to Knipsen by sundown and wearily dismounted. He eyed the saloon, but his belly protested loudly. He needed food more than he needed a shot of whiskey. Going to a small restaurant, he sat down. The chair creaked under him, echoing the way his joints felt. Being in the saddle as long as he had been over the past week was beginning to tell on him. Sleep, food, safety from men trying to kill him—he needed it all and wasn't likely to get it.

Except for the food.

"We got real good roast beef tonight. And yams. Good yams," the waiter told him.

"Bring some more," Slocum said, fishing in his pocket to see what money he had left. There was still some left. He considered what it might take to bribe his way into the Institute, and realized how little he really had. He was thinking in terms of a few dollars for whiskey and food, not large sums such as Poston had extorted to hide him for a few days.

"You have the money, mister?" asked the waiter, looking skeptical as he held out the plate.

"Got enough," Slocum said. "But what I do need is some information. I'm all confused about that place down the road a ways. The asylum."

The waiter looked as if he had bitten into something that didn't agree with him. He put the plate down in front of Slocum.

"Wish that place didn't exist."

"Isn't it good to keep the crazy people locked up rather

than wandering the countryside?" Slocum asked, knowing more of what went on inside the walls but needing to find if he had missed anything.

"Reckon that's so," the waiter said. "Since you're askin' 'bout that, you missed another service they offer." Seeing Slocum arch his eyebrow in question since his mouth was full, the waiter rambled on. "Not sayin' a God-fearin' man like you'd be interested, mind you, but they got whores there. And outlaws hidin' out. We tell the sheriff, and he ignores it."

"He being paid off?"

The waiter snorted. "What else? Lucas ain't got two nickels to rub together until that Poston fella opened the asylum. Now the sheriff's got more money than any but the most successful ranchers around here."

"Like Peter Helmann? Hear tell he's looking for cowboys. Think I could get a job there?"

"The Circle H?" The waiter shook his head. "There's somethin' strange goin' on, and from rumors, Helmann's own son had him committed to the asylum. That's somethin' else Dr. Poston is willin' to do. Put people into those fancy canvas jackets that fasten up the back, people that don't deserve it."

"You sayin' his own son sold him out? To get control of the Circle H?"

"That boy's always been a challenge," the waiter said carefully, "but last year or two he's gone plumb wild. Sorry to see Ole Pete locked up like that, but the sheriff won't do squat. The nearest judge is over in Austin, and what does he care? We're out here in the Hill Country and on our own, far as anybody in the city cares."

"Sounds like the townsfolk ought to get a posse together and tear down the front door of that place," Slocum said, seeing how agreeable the waiter was. If Slocum couldn't get in by himself, he wasn't above rustling up enough citizens to storm the gate and do what he couldn't.

"Take on those loonies?" The waiter shook his head.

From the expression on the man's face, Slocum knew the notion frightened him.

"But you said that Peter Helmann was sold up the river by his own son. That shouldn't happen. Why won't the sheriff do anything about it?"

"He's bought and paid for. So's the judge. They got a big discount on beeves from the Circle H after Ole Pete was locked up. No, sir, there's nobody in Knipsen willin' to go again' either the law or Doc Poston."

"I saw the Circle H ramrod—Billy—was getting ready for a trail drive. This is mighty early in the year to be moving a herd," Slocum said.

The waiter shrugged. "Cain't say what's goin' on out there. The Circle H is 'bout the most profitable place in Texas, 'cept for the XIT, of course."

Slocum kept eating steadily and, between bites, changed the subject again.

"That Gretchen Helmann surely is a looker," he said. This brought a smile to the waiter's face.

"Yes, sir, you said a mouthful. As purty as a summer day and just as warm."

"What would you say if I told you her brother had her locked up out at the Institute, too?"

"That's not right. I jist saw Miss Gretchen only yesterday. Here in town."

"Poston and Ludmilla took her. You can guess why, since Ludmilla is involved." Slocum didn't have to tell the waiter who Ludmilla was. The stricken look told the story. The waiter and probably every other man in Knipsen had paid a visit to the madam's quarters out at the Institute. This might be another reason no one in town was particularly interested in shutting down the asylum.

"Uwe wouldn't sell her to Dr. Poston, never," the waiter said.

"How much did he pay to have his pa locked up?"

"Heard tell as much as ten thousand dollars. It was worth it to get the Circle H, I reckon."

Slocum hurriedly finished his meal and paid. The waiter had become increasingly reticent about passing along town gossip—gossip that damned Poston. Cutting out this canker sore so close to their small town was something the sheriff ought to do, if only to get rid of the outlaw sanctuary Poston provided, but this wasn't going to happen. Slocum had hoped to recruit help other than the sheriff, anyway. It was impossible to believe that the Ranger hadn't spoken with the local lawman about the Austin bank robbery and described those he was hunting. The last thing Slocum needed was a sheriff sniffing after whatever reward the banker offered.

Food setting well in his belly, Slocum went down the street to the saloon and found a quiet spot at the corner to knock back a couple shots of whiskey. There was a half-hearted poker game going and a faro dealer who was bored from lack of players. Even the barkeep looked strangely reticent. Knipsen wasn't the kind of town where a lot happened. That made the brothel at the Institute all the more vital to the town.

Slocum had to admit that Poston ran a sweet racket. Hideout, brothel, removal of unwanted relatives. He even took in dangerous lunatics.

Knowing there was nothing to do but return to the Institute and figure out his own way inside, Slocum left the saloon and walked back toward the restaurant where he had tethered his horse. He almost stumbled when he saw Ranger Coldcreek dismounting and lashing his horse to the same iron ring Slocum had tied his horse to.

The Ranger didn't pay him any heed as he went into the restaurant. Slocum approached cautiously, pulling the reins free and leading his horse away, using it as a shield.

"Where's the posse?" asked the waiter. Slocum slowed, straining to hear the answer.

"Them boys got all het up and returned to Austin," the Ranger said. "Couldn't take more time trackin' down the varmints who robbed that bank. You haven't seen any of 'em, by any chance, have you?" The Ranger began describing Laramie and his partners. Slocum swung into the saddle by the time the Ranger got around to describing him.

He was riding hard when the Ranger shot out of the restaurant like he had been scalded. Slocum heard a steady stream of curses and then a loud protest from the lawman's horse as he mounted.

Slocum reached the outskirts of Knipsen, such as they were, and immediately cut into a grove of elm trees. The lower limbs cut and banged at his face. Slocum ducked even lower and guided his balking horse into the tangle of undergrowth, then reined back and waited. He could barely see the road from here, but made out the Ranger galloping hard. The lawman disappeared, and Slocum cautiously returned. It wouldn't be too long before the road straightened out and the Ranger realized he had passed Slocum.

Turning back to town, Slocum made his way along the main street and got on the road leading to the Breiland Institute. Getting inside to rescue both Gretchen and her father had become even harder now that Ranger Coldcreek was on his trail.

Slocum had no idea how he would get them out and keep himself from being arrested, but he would do it. He had to. Then he would get his money from Laramie and Kinsley—and that thieving Austin banker, Wilson.

11

The only good thing Slocum could say about having the Texas Ranger on his trail again was that the trail led into the Breiland Institute for the Insane. Sooner or later, no matter how slow Ranger Coldcreek might be, he had to get the idea that something about this place had to be looked at more carefully. With any luck, the Ranger might even spot Laramie or Kinsley. Considering how many people lived within the Institute walls, the Ranger might find a dozen outlaws wanted around the state hiding here.

That was the solution to a small part of his problem. More pressing was getting Gretchen Helmann away from Poston.

The wall with the barbed wire strung atop it wouldn't be much of a problem to get past. What bothered Slocum most was having to leave his horse outside the wall where the Ranger might find it. The only entry point large enough for him to ride in was the main gate, and it was effectively covered by the guard in the turret and by Gold Tooth and the others positioned in front of the Institute. Over the wall was the best way, even if he had to leave his horse.

Slocum began riding the perimeter, hunting for a spot where he wouldn't be sighted by the marksman in the turret. Less than twenty minutes later Slocum found the spot near a wooded area where he could leave his horse. He spent the rest of the afternoon napping, then made sure his horse was properly hobbled and went to the wall. A large crack in the masonry allowed him to dig his toes into the adobe bricks beneath and climb like a monkey to the top. Grabbing the barbed wire, he used the wire cutters Gretchen had given him what seemed a lifetime ago, hoisted himself up and over the top, and dropped into the walled compound. Inside the compound, he headed directly for the barn.

Twilight shadows stretched everywhere, threatening total darkness when the sun dipped far below the horizon. It would be several hours until moonrise. Slocum had to make the best of his time. Checking the barn showed a dozen horses but no stableman. He wandered about, looking for any sign that a tunnel emerged here. If he were Poston, he would want an escape tunnel to come to the spot where he could get a horse.

There might have been a dozen tunnel exits in the area, but Slocum couldn't find them. Giving up, he looked at the sprawling madhouse twenty yards away. Here and there he saw shadowy movement in the dark by the buildings. Guards. They would begin to grow careless in another four or five hours when boredom set in. Slocum didn't want to wait.

He couldn't. The pressure of time weighed too heavily on him.

Hitching up his belt, he strutted from the barn and walked directly toward the side entrance to the Institute. From his earlier hide-and-seek inside, he knew this was the entrance giving the quickest route to Poston's office. Slocum wanted to shove his six-shooter into the weasely man's belly and order him to release Gretchen and her father. That would satisfy Slocum's need to get even with the director, and it might even shake loose Laramie and Kinsley. But he had to get inside first.

Confidence and boldness got him to the side of the Institute unchallenged. But he found his first problem at the small door leading inside. It was locked.

Slocum took a look around, then figured brazenness had gotten him this far, so it ought to carry him further. He knocked.

"Let me in!" he called when he heard measured footfalls inside. "I'm late!"

"Whosit?" came the question.

"Dr. Poston will eat your heart if you don't let me in." Slocum grew impatient. The guards outside must have heard him by now. He waited to see if they poked their heads around the corner of the building. Throwing some lead in their direction was the only way he could get away if they found him now.

"Poston ain't even here," the man inside said. "I seen him go out hours back."

"Let me in," Slocum repeated. He had started to leave rather than be found by the guards when he heard the locking bar inside being pulled back. The metallic click of a heavy padlock opening finished the job of removing the barrier to getting inside.

The door opened a fraction of an inch. Slocum kicked it in and swarmed over the startled guard inside. He swung his pistol, caught the man alongside the head, and dropped him to the floor. Kicking the door shut behind him, Slocum dropped to his knees and quickly searched the unconscious guard. A ring of keys spilled out of a pocket onto the floor. Slocum snared it and stuffed it into his own pocket. Dragging the guard to a nearby room, he left the man in the center, closed and locked the door behind him. Unless another guard recognized the voice, the man inside was safely out of Slocum's hair.

He dropped the bar back into place on the exterior door, but did not fasten the padlock. If he came back this way with Gretchen and her pa, wasting time to open the padlock might mean the difference between life and death.

Slocum hurried along the corridor looking in cells both left and right. Many of the men were gibbering or outright maniacs, thrashing and banging hard into padded walls. A few wore straightjackets, but none of them was Peter Helmann or his daughter. Slocum reached Poston's office and quickly entered.

He wasn't too surprised when he saw that the man wasn't behind his big desk, although Slocum had put little store by the guard's statement that he had seen Poston leave earlier. Slocum searched the desk again, and then worked through the files on a nearby table. When he came to Peter Helmann's file, he flipped through the pages filled with bogus diagnoses. Nowhere did it show that Poston had received money to take Helmann in as a special patient. Another set of records had to be somewhere in the office—or the Institute. Slocum had never figured out where Poston slept. This was the kind of damning record Poston would hide away.

Disgusted, Slocum dropped the file back to the stack. He had to get Helmann out, and it was probably best done the same way he had gotten into the asylum. Forget the law, forget proof against Poston, get Helmann out of here. And Gretchen, too.

Slocum went to the door and looked into the lobby. The entire place was as silent as a tomb. He heard a sudden moan of an inmate that set off howling like a pack of coyotes, but this died down soon, leaving the deathly quiet. Walking as softly as possible, he crossed the lobby, looked up the stairs, and saw two guards at the landing, playing cards. They were too intent to notice him. He entered the corridor where Peter Helmann had been imprisoned before.

This time the cell was empty. Slocum cursed under his breath as he went from cell to cell, peering into each in turn. All empty. The entire wing had been evacuated.

He went back to the lobby and looked up at the two guards, wondering how far he could get bulling his way up. If he couldn't get Peter Helmann freed, he had to find

Gretchen. His foot touched the first step up when he heard the front door behind him opening.

"Who're you?" called Gold Tooth. "What're you doin' down here?"

Slocum prepared to draw and fire when he heard a soft whishing of skirts and found himself engulfed by feminine arms and a questing red-lipped mouth eager to kiss him.

"Oh, he is mine!" cooed Ludmilla.

"You let him in?" asked Gold Tooth. Past the madam's tangle of piled hair, Slocum saw that Gold Tooth had two other guards with him.

"He is an old customer, *da,*" she said. "You naughty boy. You must give Ludmilla warning, so I can be beautiful for you."

"He's a personal client?" Gold Tooth grinned so much, what light there was in the lobby caught his tooth and turned it into a small sun. Slocum suspected that Gold Tooth was a mite jealous.

Slocum kept his face buried in Ludmilla's hair, then moved to kiss her neck and work his face down into her ample cleavage.

"Oh, naughty, naughty boy, not here," she said, stroking over his arms and letting her fingers eventually press into his chest. She said one thing and did another. Slocum wondered if she would let him take her on the stairs with the guards watching. Probably.

"Upstairs?" he asked. His voice was muffled by the folds of her dress and the twin mounds of her pillowy breasts.

"But of course, soon, oh, soon," she said. He felt her sag a little. Taking her cue, Slocum got his arms under her legs and around her shoulders. With a swoop, he caught her up and began carrying her up the stairs.

"You want us to—" began Gold Tooth.

"I want you to leave me to my customers," Ludmilla said, shooing him away as if he were some sort of small child. Slocum didn't have to turn to know Gold Tooth fol-

lowed her orders. He heard the double door click shut.
Gold Tooth was the grounds guard, not one watching the
inmates.

"Where's Jonah?" Slocum asked.

"Why do you ask? You want *him*?" Ludmilla teased
him. She batted her long black eyelashes and stared boldly
at him.

"Only you," Slocum said. "I wanted to have him bring
us some wine."

"I will serve," Ludmilla said. "I will make you giddy
with the wine I serve!"

"Just being this close makes me giddy," Slocum said,
sweeping past the guards. Both men looked up from their
cards but never got a good look at him. Even if they had, he
didn't know if they would connect him with the earlier intruder. Jonah wasn't the kind to give good descriptions,
and Poston had an entire Institute to run. Slocum need
worry only if Laramie or Kinsley spotted him.

"You say such sweet nothings," Ludmilla sighed. She
tightened her grip around his neck and began kissing.

Slocum got to the third floor and put her feet back onto
the floor. She kept her arms around his neck and never
stopped kissing. He got a quick look around. There weren't
any of the other ladies of easy virtue in sight.

"I have a special request," Slocum said.

"Ah, you want this?" Ludmilla dropped to her knees in
front of him and began unfastening the buttons of his fly.
He reached down and stopped her.

"I want something else. Someone else," he said. "Not
that I wasn't fine with you, but I've had a real hankering for
blondes lately. Real blondes. Not ones wearing wigs or doing fancy things to make their hair color different."

Ludmilla's expression went from one of lust to avarice.
She pouted prettily and pretended to be hurt.

"I am not so good enough for you?"

"Don't get me wrong. I'm not the Czar of Russia who
wants to get rid of you for political reasons. Maybe after-

ward, we could spend time together. But you're not a blonde," Slocum said. "I'm looking for something fresh and innocent. Maybe a bit feisty, too."

"I have one who will not just lie under you. It will be the bucking bronco. She is fierce. So fierce she is tied down."

"This sounds . . . intriguing," Slocum said as he tried to strike a balance between feigned indifference and outright enthusiasm. His heart beat a little faster. If Ludmilla had brought Gretchen here, she would have the woman locked up. Why not tied down somewhere close? His mind raced ahead as he planned how to free her and then together they could find her father.

"You are sure?" Ludmilla reached out and stroked over the bulge in his jeans. "I know things you might never have seen. Russian things."

"After," Slocum said uneasily. He was responding to the lovely woman's caresses. "Thinking of a blonde—the right one—is doing things to me."

"I am not doing these things?" Ludmilla looked up, her eyes blazing with hunger. Slocum wondered if it was hunger for what he had to offer behind his fly or in his wallet. He found out quickly enough.

"One hundred dollars," Ludmilla said. "You can have me for less, but this one, this blonde, she is only here soon."

"Newly arrived?"

"*Da*," Ludmilla said. She rocked back and got to her feet. The woman pressed closer to Slocum so he could look down her décolleté. A shimmy rubbed her breasts against his chest; then she whirled away as gracefully as a ballet dancer. Looking back over her shoulder, she reached out and left her open palm just above her shoulder.

Slocum fumbled through the wad of greenbacks and peeled off a few dollars, almost all he had. If paying led him to Gretchen, it was worth it.

"This way," Ludmilla said. She had quite a hitch in her git-along. Slocum knew she rolled her hips and made more exaggerated steps to punish him for not hopping into bed with her. Ludmilla stopped in front of a door just off the sitting room and pushed it open.

Slocum saw a woman sitting on a bed, half-dressed and looking completely drunk.

"No," he said. "Not innocent-looking enough for me."

"But Betty is blond and so good. Not as good as me, but—"

"She's not blond," Slocum said as the whore on the bed turned and spread her legs in what she thought was wanton invitation. "And she's not all that feisty."

"Ah, the bucking bronco," Ludmilla said. "I forgot."

Slocum knew the madam forgot nothing. She was playing with him.

"This way," Ludmilla said, reaching down and gripping his crotch. She tugged, and he followed all the way to the end of the short corridor. A window opened onto the roof where he had slipped and slid his way out before. Slocum vowed not to take that route again, unless all other ways were closed to him. He had been lucky once falling off the roof. He might break a leg if he tried it again. And with Gretchen, it was too much to think they could both get to the ground from here.

"This is more like it," Slocum said when Ludmilla opened the bedroom door with a dramatic gesture. Stretched spread-eagle on the bed lay a struggling Gretchen Helmann. She grumbled constantly around the gag stuffed into her mouth. When she saw him, she fought against the ropes holding her wrists and ankles with even more fury, but the look in her eyes told Slocum she knew the real reason he was here.

"I thought this to be so," Ludmilla said triumphantly.

"Hey, wait," Slocum said. The Russian madam had stepped behind him, reached around, and deftly unfastened his gun belt. She swung it out of his grip.

"You do not need these to be with her," Ludmilla said.

"Reckon not," Slocum said. "I feel naked without the six-shooter."

"I like to feel you naked," Ludmilla said. She didn't notice that Gretchen stopped her fake struggles on the bed at these words. Ludmilla kissed him, then stepped back into the hall. "You will enjoy your innocent one, then come to me to see what experience does."

Ludmilla closed the door. Slocum heard the lock click into place, but he wasn't worried. He still had the knife thrust into the top of his boot. In a little while he could knock on the door and Ludmilla would open it and he would overpower her. First, he and Gretchen needed to make plans to find her father and then escape.

Slocum plucked the gag from Gretchen's mouth. Her blue eyes were wide.

"We can—"

"Shut up!" Gretchen's outburst caught him by surprise. The woman hastily whispered, "She's listening and watching. There's a peephole on the door."

Slocum looked up at the mirror over the bed and shifted on the bed beside Gretchen until it reflected the inside of the bedroom door. Slocum saw the peephole. He had no reason to believe that Gretchen was wrong about Ludmilla watching. It was the kind of thing the horny madam would do.

"I have to get you out of here. I'll cut your ropes and—"

"No! She warned me about trying to escape. She'll call that hulk of a guard again." Gretchen shuddered as she remembered what Jonah must have done to her. "I hate her—and she kissed you. She sounded like you and her—"

"That's her job," Slocum said quickly, "to sound friendly to men. I was lucky to find you so fast. I saw them kidnap you in town but couldn't rescue you along the road."

"I wanted to die, but then I thought I wanted to kill them all more!"

Slocum appreciated Gretchen's determination, but it did nothing to get her free.

"Ludmilla said she'd call Jonah if you got free of the ropes? Even if I freed you?"

"She's watching. If . . . if she doesn't see what she expects to see, she'll call the guards," Gretchen said.

"You know what she expects to see. I paid her."

"Really?"

"Don't think you're worth that much?" Slocum said, smiling. She was an alluring woman, blond hair in wild disarray on the pillow framing her oval face like a picture frame. And the picture was beautiful. As Gretchen breathed a little faster, her breasts rose and fell. They pressed hard against her shirt until the hard nubbins of her nipples poked into the cloth.

"If you paid her . . ." Gretchen licked her lips and half closed her eyes. "You'd better get your money's worth," she said. "While she's watching."

Slocum felt a shiver of anticipation at Gretchen's words.

"Are you sure?"

"Yes," she said. Her eyes went wide and then half closed again. Gretchen wiggled on the bed, held by the ropes but still able to put enough into the motion to entice Slocum.

He bent over and kissed her. He wanted it to be gentle. She raised up and crushed her lips into his. Then she bit him hard enough to cause his lip to bleed.

"You pig!" she shrieked. Lower, she said, "Go on, do it. You have to."

Slocum knew she might be right about having to continue, but he also wanted to. It didn't bother him that Ludmilla was spying on them. All he could think about was Gretchen tied on the bed.

"I could let you free of those ropes," he said loud enough for Ludmilla to overhear. Gretchen began undulating on the bed, causing the springs to squeak. "But I won't. I'll leave you tied down. Hog-tied, like a scrappy calf."

He bent and kissed her again. This time she didn't bite him. Her lips parted and her pink tongue flashed out to lightly touch where she had bitten him, as if she could kiss the injury and make it well. Slocum reached down and pressed his hands into her breasts. He felt the heavy beat of her heart through her shirt.

"Open it. Kiss them. Make it look real," Gretchen whispered.

"Real?" Slocum laughed. "It's real what I feel." He did as she told him, unbuttoning the blonde's blouse until her snowy breasts were exposed. Pink nips pulsed with visible lust. He sucked first one and then the other into his mouth, licked and kissed until it was ruddy and then moved on. He dived into the canyon between those succulent mounds, and then worked lower until he came to the waistband of her skirt.

"Don't undo it. Scrunch it up around my waist. I . . . I don't have bloomers on."

Slocum lifted her skirts and slowly exposed her strong legs. He moved upward until he came to the tangled bush hidden between her thighs. Crinkly golden fur guarded the fleshy gates to her inner sanctum. He stroked over her nether lips and felt ripples of desire pass through Gretchen's supple young body. Several strokes later his hand came away oily with her inner juices. He stood and dropped his jeans.

Her eyes fluttered open as she stared at his hardness. She caught her breath and whispered, "yes."

He got onto the bed and positioned himself between her wide-spread legs. Reaching down, he cupped her firm buttocks and lifted her off the bed enough so he could enter her.

She began struggling against the ropes, tossing her head and moaning. He pushed forward slowly, parting those lips he had stroked with his fingers, moving deeper into her heated center. When he was entirely within her, he paused. She was bucking and flailing about. He couldn't tell if it was an act for Ludmilla's benefit or it was from the fleshy spike within her.

When she tightened around him and he almost lost control, he knew Gretchen wasn't faking her passion. Gripping with both hands, he lifted her again and slowly withdrew. Then he thrust forward. The heat, the tightness, the sight of the lovely woman bound and aroused spurred him on.

Her breasts flopped about just inches away. Slocum bent forward and lightly kissed each of them, then felt her clamp down hard all around him. This was all she could do. Her hands and feet were secured to the four bedposts too securely for much movement. She could lift and drop— and she could grip down all around his steely shaft. And she did.

He felt as if he were being milked by an expert. The rhythmic movement sent jabs of delight into his loins.

"More, more," Gretchen gasped out. He began stroking with long, powerful strokes that lifted her off the bed and strained the ropes. "Yes, oh, yes!"

A powerful convulsion seized Gretchen and caused her to clamp down powerfully along his entire hidden length. Slocum could not keep going much longer. Everything about the woman and her helplessness excited him. Her obvious passion and desire for him pushed him over the edge. The white-hot tide built within his body, slowly edged along his shaft, and then exploded with a fury that rocked him.

Gretchen arched her back, shoved her hips upward to meet him, and shrieked in release as he spilled his seed into her. Then they sank back to the bed, Slocum's weight pressing down on her so their lips were close.

"I'm sorry," Slocum said.

"I'm not," Gretchen panted out. "It . . . it's never been like this for me before."

"What are we going to do to get out?"

"Is that witch still spying on us?"

Slocum looked up at the mirror over the bed, but couldn't tell. He backed away, looked down at the mostly naked Gretchen, and felt a new twitch. He ignored it as he got off the bed, pulled up his jeans, and went to the door. The peephole was closed.

He heaved a sigh. Ludmilla had watched long enough to sate her own desire and had gone off. Whether she'd gone to fetch other girls to spy on Slocum and Gretchen or she'd called the guards, he didn't know. She might simply be waiting for him in the sitting room, ready to collect her own roll in the hay.

"Well?"

Slocum turned and saw the expression on Gretchen's face.

"Are you going to cut me free?"

"That wasn't what you were telling me to do a few minutes ago."

"That was a few minutes ago," Gretchen said. She watched as he slashed the ropes. She fell limp to the bed, the circulation in her hands and feet gone from being bound so long.

Slocum rubbed her wrists until she pushed him away. Then he rubbed her ankles until her toes curled.

"That's good," she said primly. "There's no need to continue."

"I enjoy it," Slocum said, grinning at her. "Don't you?" He didn't get the answer he expected.

"Yes," she said in a husky voice, sitting up and giving him a big, wet kiss. Her naked breasts rubbed against his chest as she clung to him.

"We've got to get out of here," he told her. "Find your father, get him free, and then all of us get out of here."

"How?" Gretchen asked.

Slocum didn't have any idea how they would get away. But something would come to him. It had to if they were going to escape with their lives from the heart of the Breiland Institute for the Insane.

12

It took Slocum only a few seconds to find that Ludmilla had locked them into the room. He dropped to his knees and pressed his eye against the metal of the lock. All he saw was the key thrust into the keyhole from outside.

"Can you get us out? We can knock the door down," Gretchen said. She started to slam into it with her shoulder. Slocum stopped her.

"There's a better way. Is there a sheet of paper anywhere?"

"No, I don't think so. You figure folks'd come to a whorehouse to read?"

Slocum grabbed a sheet from the bed.

"This will do," he said. He pressed it flat and slid it under the door. With a quick move, he pulled his knife from its sheath and poked the tip against the key. It grated a bit, then fell to the floor in the hall. Slocum quickly pulled the sheet back in under the door. The key gleamed in the middle of the sheet.

"That's remarkable," Gretchen said, admiration shining in her bright eyes. "You have more talents than what you just showed me a few minutes ago." As the words came from her lips, she blushed and turned away. Slocum had to smile. She was a curious blend of innocent and wanton. That appealed a lot to Slocum.

He shoved the key into the lock and turned. The grating sound seemed deafening, but Slocum knew it was hardly audible a few feet away. He only hoped that Ludmilla was farther away than that. Opening the door, he chanced a quick look out. Ludmilla stood in the middle of the sitting room, her arms wrapped around a man and kissing him hard. Slocum closed the door and stood.

"She's likely to be occupied for a spell," Slocum said. "This is our chance to sneak out." He was worried that the other Cyprians would not be as engrossed in their work as Ludmilla, but going out to the roof and down to the grounds was out of the question. Surviving the drop a second time was possible, but that put them outside the Institute when Peter Helmann was locked up inside.

"I'd rip out her eyes, if I could," Gretchen said with heat. Slocum looked at her and wondered if she was jealous. It had been obvious what had gone on between Ludmilla and Slocum earlier. He started to explain, then bit back the words. He had no reason to explain anything to Gretchen Helmann. He was helping her get her pa out of this madhouse. Whatever it required, Slocum was willing to do.

"Here," he said, pulling the derringer from his coat pocket. He held it out for her. The blaze of emotion in Gretchen's eyes as she took it made him worry he had made a mistake. He had no worry that Gretchen would accidentally fire it. She looked capable with the two-shot pistol or probably any firearm. Her judgment when to use it wore more heavily on Slocum. Then he shrugged it off.

He opened the door, and saw that Ludmilla and her paramour had vanished. He motioned Gretchen to follow. When she was outside, he closed and locked the door.

"Let her figure out how we escaped," he said softly. After the key was left in the same position in the lock as it had been before he knocked it to the floor, he slipped into the sitting room. To his right a door stood partially open.

"She's—"

"Quiet," Slocum cautioned. This was Ludmilla's room, and the man she entertained was none other than Laramie. "We've got other fish to fry." He started looking around the room for his gun belt and Colt Navy.

"This what you want?" asked Gretchen, holding up the holster. The six-shooter was still securely tucked into it. Slocum silently took it and strapped it around his waist. With the familiar heft at his left hip, he felt as if he could lick his weight in wildcats.

If Ludmilla saw him, that was exactly how he would have to fight.

They crossed the room to the stairs leading down to the second-floor landing. Other doors were ajar. Sounds of the women entertaining the paying "inmates" told Slocum it was past the dinner hour, the time when the men would get restless and want female companionship. He hoped they were entitled to all-night privileges with the women. That would keep most of his problems safely out of the way as he hunted for Peter Helmann.

"Aren't you going to do something?" Gretchen asked. She looked outraged.

"We are doing something," he said, puzzled at what she meant. "We're finding your pa."

"But them! Th-they're making—doing—"

"Laramie and his partner Kinsley are not going to notice me as long as Ludmilla and her girls have them distracted. Now shut up and come along." Slocum was losing his patience with her. Gretchen started to reply angrily, then gripped the derringer tightly and only glared at him.

Step by step Slocum went down the stairs to a point where he could see the two men still playing cards. He had gotten past them because of Ludmilla being with him. An idea came to him. Slocum grabbed Gretchen around the waist and swung her around, whispering in her ear, "Play along."

He kissed her. She tried to push away, then melted in his arms. He kissed her again as he went down the steps and came into view of the two guards.

"Somewhere more exciting, sweetheart," he said loud enough for the guards to hear. "I want to do it somewhere other than in a bed."

Gretchen's acquiescence evaporated, and she tried to push away. He held her close so the men couldn't see his face.

"How dare you!" she hissed.

"A wonderful idea," Slocum said loudly. "The office is empty right now."

"Hey, mister, you be careful. Dr. Poston ain't due back for a spell, but he wouldn't take kindly to you and her messin' up his desk, if you know what I mean."

"Don't worry," Slocum said, as much to Gretchen as to the men. "This won't take long at all."

"Then maybe you can share her," said the guard. "She's 'bout the purtiest in Ludmilla's whole stable, and that includes the old bitch herself!"

"See?" Slocum said softly. "You're appreciated."

He grunted when Gretchen tried to knee him in the groin. This produced guffaws from the guards. Slocum hurried the blonde down the stairs to the deserted lobby. He released her. Gretchen spun away, her face livid with anger.

"This is only a joke to you! A game! A humiliating game!"

"Won't it be worth it if you and your pa get out of here in one piece?"

"I—" Gretchen clamped her mouth shut as she glared at him. He watched as her expression turned softer again. Maybe she remembered what they had done upstairs and remembered how she had liked it. Or maybe he had appealed to her sense of duty. It didn't matter. She wasn't going to try to knee him in the balls again.

"Good. Your father was in a cell down that corridor when I was here before," Slocum said, "but he's not there. Where do you think they'd take him?"

"How should I know? I have never been in this horrible place."

Slocum let her protest all she wanted. It kept her busy while he thought through the problem of where to find Peter Helmann. If a regular cell wasn't safe enough to hold him any longer, somewhere secret would be. The tunnels under the Institute where Slocum had found the skeletons still chained to the walls were the most likely—and frightening—place to put an inmate they wanted to ignore.

"Come on," Slocum said. He glanced toward the lobby, worried that Poston and Jonah might return at any moment. Or the guards on the upper landing would get suspicious and come after them. Worse, he had given them reason to become curious about what amorous activities he and Gretchen might engage in on the director's desk. The Institute wasn't a place that valued privacy very highly.

He reached the end of the corridor where he had opened the trapdoor to the lower tunnels and took one last look around. Going down this ladder meant exposing Gretchen to some grisly deaths, but there was no way to avoid it. He had seen how tough she could be. How tough she would be if they found her father chained and dead was another matter. Slocum considered taking the derringer from her before they descended, then saw the way she clutched it like a lifeline. Getting it away from her now would be harder than dealing with her if they found her pa.

Grunting, he pushed the desk to one side and pulled up the heavy trapdoor.

"Why is this here?" she asked. Slocum didn't answer. She would find out soon enough.

He dropped down, found the sturdiest rung, and quickly

descended to the tunnel floor. By the time Gretchen joined him, he had his remaining lucifers out and ready to use.

"The door," she said. "It should not be left open." She started back up, but Slocum stopped her.

"Listen," he said. The steady click of boots against the corridor floor echoed along and down the hole. "Somebody's coming."

"We must shoot them!"

"We must run like hell," he said. Slocum glanced back up and wondered if the guard would reach the end of the corridor. The desk meant a guard was usually posted there. They might have been lucky and the guard had been off taking a leak, but now that luck had run out.

He set off, not bothering to strike a match. One hand against the cold damp stone wall, Slocum walked as fast as he could. There weren't open pits along the tunnels, but enough debris littered the bottom to make the going dangerous in the dark.

"Wait, John, not so fast," Gretchen protested.

"The guard'll find the trapdoor open and raise an alarm. He might think an inmate is loose, but we can't take the risk. If Ludmilla checks and finds us gone, they'll search the entire asylum for us."

Slocum blundered along until he felt the tunnel turn. Only then did he strike a lucifer. Gretchen gasped when she saw a skeleton dangling from chains in an alcove next to her.

"That is . . ."

"Not your pa," Slocum said harshly. "Come on. No time to waste." It might have been his imagination, but he fancied he heard boots scrapping against wood—like feet going down the ladder rungs behind them.

"It is so barbaric," Gretchen said. She gasped again when they passed an even more decayed body in shackles, but she fell silent when they came to a niche with a newly dead body. Slocum hesitated when he saw it, but had to look. He grabbed the hair on the corpse's head and lifted.

He glanced back at Gretchen and saw her face. Shock etched every lovely line of her face, but there was no recognition. He let the head flop down, satisfied this was not Peter Helmann.

Slocum hurried on, dropping the lucifer when it burned down to his fingers. He had found a branching corridor that he didn't remember from his earlier brief exploration. When he saw the dancing light of a torch far behind them in the corridor, he knew his ears hadn't played tricks on him. At least one guard had come down to explore the underground maze of tunnels.

"This way," he said, making a quick decision.

"Where's it go?" Gretchen asked. Slocum didn't answer because she would not like it that he had no idea where they went. Away from their pursuers. That was good enough for the time being. When he found another branching tunnel, he took it, going at a slight angle to their original tunnel. Within a few minutes they had eluded their pursuer—and Slocum had gotten so turned around he was completely lost.

Slocum stopped suddenly when he realized his plight. Gretchen bumped into him, her arms circling him to keep her balance.

"Sorry," she said. Where she had inadvertently grabbed him would have been fine under other circumstances. Her hands lingered a tad longer than if she had been truly sorry.

"We can't keep blundering around in the dark," Slocum said. "I've only got a couple lucifers left."

"John!" Gretchen clutched at his arm now. "Men. Talking!"

He heard them. Their pursuers made no effort to keep their voices down, as much to spook those they pursued as to bolster their own courage. Slocum heard just a hint of fear in those guards as they spoke to one another. He felt their fear, too. The dark, the dead, chained bodies, the potential for instant death all wore on any man's nerves.

"I don't want to gun them down," he said, "since I don't

know how many there are. If they trap us between two groups, we're dead." He tapped the chains of the nearby corpse to emphasize what he meant. He felt Gretchen begin to shake.

"I want to get out of here, John. I want out!"

"After we find your pa," he said. Slocum wasn't going to get out of the Breiland Institute for the Insane only to have to return another time to get Helmann. He tugged on her arm as they made their way down the pitch-black tunnel. Slocum jumped when a drop of cold water dripped onto his face. It made him feel a bit foolish, jumping at this small thing in the dark, but everything about these underground passageways made him jittery.

"John," Gretchen said, pulling away from him. "I've found something. I think it's a ladder."

Slocum homed in on her voice in the dark, aware of how the dancing light from the guards' torch was coming closer. They were in the crossing corridor, but would look down this one and see their two fugitives. The notion hit Slocum that they weren't sure how many people were ahead of them. He might hide Gretchen and take on the guards. Then he felt her fingers grip his wrist and guide him to the wood ladder.

"Up," he decided. He had no idea where this led, but it got them away from the guards.

"Another trapdoor, John. I can't budge it."

He swarmed up the ladder and felt it begin to sag under their combined weight. Getting around Gretchen, he put his shoulder to the door and began applying pressure. The rung under his foot broke. He moved higher.

"What's that? Somebody *is* down here," cried a guard.

Slocum cursed their bad luck. The guards hadn't been certain until now that they were after anyone running around the tunnels. Now they were on Slocum and Gretchen's trail.

"Got it," Slocum said, feeling the trapdoor yielding. He surged upward again and sent the trapdoor flying open to bang against the floor. He and Gretchen made their way through, then he closed it. Breathing hard, he hadn't realized how spooked he had been down in those corpse-lined tunnels.

"Where are we?" Gretchen asked. She looked around. They had come up in a grim, dank corridor. The stench added to the sense that people here died. Often. A low drone came from down the hall, a sound that Slocum struggled to make sense of. Words—almost words—flitted at the edge of his mind.

"Go look," Slocum said. "I'll check the other direction." He ran to the end of the corridor and found an iron door secured on the other side. A small grate in the door afforded him a narrow view of the room on the other side. Two guards slept at a table, their heads resting on folded arms as they snored loudly. One talked in his sleep. Slocum saw the key ring on the table between them. He stepped back and studied the door. It would take more than a battering ram to open from this side.

He went cold inside when it hit him what the droning noise was coming from the other end of the corridor.

Running hard, he caught up with Gretchen as she opened the heavy door onto a room filled with inmates. Real inmates. None of the men inside the room had paid to be here to hide from the law. Dressed in formless canvas smocks, they stared at blank stone walls, shouted at one another in languages no human tongue could get around, made tiny trapped-animal sounds, did myriad things no sane person ever would.

"Bedlam," Gretchen said in a choked voice. "We've stumbled onto the lowest level of hell."

He started to close the door. None of the inmates had noticed them. He stopped when he saw the trapdoor they had entered this corridor by begin to lift.

He drew his six-shooter, and then realized how futile it would be to shoot it out. They were trapped with the inmates, the only way out back down the trapdoor. One guard poked his head up, then he scampered out. Another and another followed. The last one shouted down into the underground passage, "You fellas wait down there. If they came this way, it won't take long to find 'em."

Slocum pushed Gretchen into the room with the lunatics. If everyone in the room chose, they could overpower the guards and escape. He saw quickly that it would be impossible to turn more than one or two of the more violent inmates against the guards.

"What are we going to do?" Gretchen was frantic.

"Blend in," Slocum said. He grabbed a canvas smock like those worn by the inmates from a wood peg by the door and tossed it to her. A larger one slipped easily around his shoulders. He took off his hat and stuffed it under the flapping fabric, then grabbed the edges and pulled them together to hide his clothing and especially his gun belt. Slocum saw that Gretchen had put on her smock with some distaste. Her nose wrinkled.

"Lice," she said, uneasily moving around.

"In here. The door's not locked," a guard outside said.

Slocum motioned for Gretchen to pull the smock up over her head to hide her blond hair. Even after everything she had been through, it was a silky, golden cascade compared with the other inmates' short-cropped hair. Hiding that she was a woman amid the ill-kempt men wasn't as much a problem because of the voluminous canvas smock. She turned and hoisted the back of the smock up as a guard poked his head into the room.

"Just a bunch of loonies," he said. Slocum hunkered down to the floor and tried to imitate the man next to him, rocking to and fro and muttering to himself.

Gretchen had turned away, but she jumped. Slocum guessed that the lice were beginning to feast on her tender flesh. He rested his hand on the butt of his six-gun when Gretchen began yelping and dancing around, drawing unwanted attention to herself.

"What's goin' on?" The guard came into the room. Two others trailed him.

Gretchen kept her face away and bent double to hide her blond hair from them, but she couldn't keep from bucking, jerking around, and letting out tiny yelps as the lice feasted on her.

"Go see what's wrong," the lead guard said to the other on his right.

Slocum let his smock open slightly so he could swing his six-shooter out, but he froze. Other inmates began to dance around with Gretchen, yelping as she had and bobbing around like leaves in a millrace.

"Never mind," said the lead guard. "Let the loonies enjoy their barn dance. We gotta find whoever was in the tunnel. They must still be down there."

"They couldn't be," piped up the third guard. "The trap was open."

"Keep your trap shut, Lou," snapped the lead guard. "They musta seen what was here, retreated, and left the trapdoor open to decoy us. But you're too dumb to see that, ain't ya?"

Slocum chanced a better look as the three guards left, arguing among themselves. He heaved a sigh of relief. Then his heart jumped into his throat. The guards locked the door behind them. Slocum and Gretchen were trapped in the large cell with a dozen lunatics.

13

Slocum grabbed at the handle on the door and tugged hard. Locked. He pushed his face against the grille, but there was a sliding plate on the other side that blocked his view. The guards might be on the other side of the door laughing, knowing they had trapped him and Gretchen. He shoved the gun to the grille and almost called out, wanting one of the guards to open the slide so he could blow his brains out. The gloating would be the last thing to cross his brain before the slug ripped out the gray matter and splashed it on the far wall.

But Slocum hesitated. He was experiencing unusual panic because of the others locked in the room with him. They were all crazy as bedbugs and being trapped with them put him on edge.

"They locked us in," Gretchen said, still slapping at her arms and legs and occasionally pressing into her body to crush the lice infesting her smock. She saw that Slocum wasn't moving. She ripped off the smock and threw it to the floor. The lunatics saw her and duplicated her effort, ripping off their clothing. She turned away when it became apparent more than one of them was not stopping until they were bare-ass.

117

"Get us out, John, get us out of here now!" Gretchen was crying. "Please," she said in a choked voice. "I can't stand another minute of this."

Slocum slid his six-shooter back into its holster and pressed his ear against the metal door. Any movement out in the corridor would be magnified, and he could tell if the guards were still there, laughing at their cleverness in catching their quarry. Slocum heard nothing.

"They don't know we're here. That's in our favor."

"What else is in our favor?"

Slocum smiled crookedly as he said, "You're the belle of the ball." The inmates were still dancing around, four of them stark naked, in the same fashion Gretchen had when she was plucking away the nits chewing on her on her fine skin.

She let out a tiny laugh and shook her head.

"I never much liked barn dances. If I get to one after this, I'll dance the soles off my shoes."

Slocum listened with half an ear as he stepped back and looked at the wall around the door. The masonry was in good repair, and the door hinges were on the outside. He tapped the solid door and listened to the dull ring that told him rust hadn't weakened it.

"I can get us out," he said with more confidence than he felt. He drew his knife and worked it between the doorjamb and the door, lifting slowly until he felt resistance. Grabbing the hilt with both hands, Slocum began straining. The angle was wrong, he lacked leverage—and the locking bar on the other side of the door popped free of its support. A clatter loud enough to cause Gretchen to jump echoed up and down the corridor. Slocum wasted no time swinging open the door and stepping out, six-shooter drawn and ready for action.

Empty. The corridor was empty and the two sleeping guards beyond the other locked door were still asleep.

"Where are the men who followed us?" asked Gretchen, pressing close behind.

"Close and bar the door," Slocum said. His eyes fixed on the trapdoor in the floor. The guards who had locked them with the lunatics must have gone back down into the tunnels to continue their search. He wasn't sure if this was a good thing.

"You don't have to tell me twice," Gretchen said. She pushed one of the naked men back into the room as he tried to get out, slammed the door, and shoved her shoulder against it. The locking bar dropped back into place, securing the inmates once more in their private hell.

"Check the other rooms," Slocum said.

"To be sure those doors are locked?"

"For your pa," he said. It was easy to forget why he had come to the Institute—why he had come back a third time—when men intending to kill them chased them through tunnels and locked them in cells.

"Oh," Gretchen said in a tiny voice. "I'd almost forgotten." In a stronger voice she said, "Do you think he's here?"

"I don't know how many cells they have, but it can't be as many as it looks from the outside, not with a working whorehouse upstairs and quarters for outlaws paying to hide out."

"Whorehouse," grumbled Gretchen, still furious at what Ludmilla had done to her. "Ought to cut her heart out, that one. And Poston! He's worst of all!"

Slocum let her go from cell to cell, peering in as she hunted for her father, while he returned to the door leading to the guardroom. One of the men stirred, stretched, and yawned widely. His partner also stirred. Slocum swung out of view through the tiny grille in the door. He checked his pocket watch, surprised to find that it was about an hour until dawn. The two guards had slept on duty, and now had to wake up enough to greet their replacements.

"John!"

He glanced over his shoulder. Gretchen frantically motioned for him to join her.

"It's my papa. He's in this cell, but he's all chained up!"

Slocum looked into the cell and saw the same man he had spoken with earlier. He felt some small vindication that he had found Peter Helmann before, but getting him out of the cell now was going to be hard. The door was barred, but opening that was simple since they were on the proper side. The shackles binding him, though, were another matter. They shone brightly, brand-new steel bracelets and locks.

"Go to him," Slocum said. "I'll see what I can do." He returned to the door leading to the guardroom. Both men were now moving around, forcing Slocum to keep out of sight since, at any instant, they might glance toward the grating and spot him.

"They gonna take out the garbage today?" asked one.

"Yeah, any time now. It's sunup, so the crew oughta be here."

"We don't have to move them, do we? It always gives me the creeps bein' round dead bodies."

"You stay out of the tunnels, then," taunted the other guard. He laughed at the first one's uneasiness with the bodies below. "They left 'em for a reason there, but up here, they gotta get rid of 'em."

"Yeah, yeah, they collect money from the county," said the other. "I heard it all. Poston gets money, but we don't. It ain't fair. We do the dirty work, and he gets the money."

"It's not that much. Only ten dollars a body."

Slocum slipped back to the cell where Gretchen knelt beside the chained man, speaking in a low voice. They both looked at him when he joined them.

"How do we open the shackles?" Gretchen asked anxiously.

Slocum confirmed his earlier guess about the quality of the chains and locks. He shook his head.

"We'd need keys, and those are probably outside with the guards."

"So shoot them!" Gretchen cried. "Shoot them and take the key and—"

"Wrong side of the locked door," Peter Helmann grated out. His voice sounded like a rusty hinge. He tried to touch his daughter, but his hand shook uncontrollably. Slocum saw that getting him out of the Institute was going to be a chore, even if they got the shackles off his wrists and ankles.

"What? Oh, you mean if John shot them, we'd still have to open the door between us." Gretchen frowned, then brightened. "We decoy them to open the door, then shoot them down and get their keys."

"There are more joining them any minute," Slocum said. "They're coming in to do something I didn't catch." He hefted his six-shooter and considered shooting off the locks. Four locks meant he'd only have two rounds left when the guards came rushing in to see what the ruckus was. He might be able to cut them down, as bloodthirsty Gretchen wanted, but it was cutting it too close.

Shooting a couple rounds might bring them both rushing in. He could get outside and grab the keys, but the shots would alert the other guards hunting through the tunnels for them. Any firearm discharge now would bring down the wrath of the entire Institute on their heads. There had to be something else he could do to get them out. What it was baffled him. Even if Peter Helmann were free of the chains, he could not walk unsupported. As much as Gretchen would assure him that she could carry her father while they escaped, Slocum doubted it.

"Keep working on the chains. Here," Slocum said, handing her his knife. He doubted she would make any progress, but it kept her busy and buoyed Helmann's spirits while Slocum investigated the rest of this wing of cells. There had to be another way out, other than into the tunnels. Still, if Slocum could not figure a way out, they had to reenter the underground corridors and probably shoot it out with the guards.

He worked from cell to cell until he came to the far end. The stench rising from one cell caused his nose to wrinkle.

Slocum opened the door and saw three corpses stretched out on tables. From the way the bodies were dressed, they were inmates who had died. From the gut-turning smell, they had died within the past few days and were turning putrid. He backed from the cell and started to explore further when an idea hit him. Slocum returned to the cell and saw heavy canvas bags piled in the corner intended for carrying bodies.

Things began falling into place for him. The guards were talking about a burial detail. The undertaker or his assistants would come here, pick up the bodies, and probably take them immediately to a graveyard.

Slocum ran back down the corridor to Helmann's cell. He poked his head inside and said, "Never mind trying to get the shackles off. Help him down the hall, last door on the right."

"Th-that's where they p-put the bodies," Helmann said.

"You're going to be carried out of here in style," Slocum said. "All you have to do is play dead. Get him down there *now*."

Slocum ran back to the cell and sucked in a deep breath, holding it as he grabbed two of the canvas bags and worked to wrestle the decaying bodies into them. He had to gasp for breath now and then, but he worked with a will. By the time he had the second body stuffed into its bag, Gretchen helped Peter Helmann into the cell.

"You'll have to pretend to be dead," Slocum said. "You go into the bag, they carry you out, they drive you to a cemetery. We'll get you away from them then."

"They're not guards," Helmann said. "They work in Knipsen. Grave diggers."

"That's what I thought. They won't put up a fuss if somebody sticks a gun into their faces."

"But they are expecting only three bodies," Helmann said. "If I get in, there'll be four."

"Only three canvas bags," Slocum said. "Get into it, and

Gretchen, you might wrap his chains in cloth to keep them from rattling."

"But he's right, John. What—oh," she said in a small voice. It came to her what Slocum had to do about the time he got his arms around the third corpse and hoisted it up and slung it over his shoulder.

It felt as if he carried a bag of suet, only no suet had ever smelled so bad. Slocum doubted he would be able to wash the death stink off his clothing or skin, but there was no way around dealing directly with the body. He twisted through the cell door and hurried down to Peter Helmann's old cell. Placing the body in such a way that its face was away from the door and its arms and legs hidden, it might fool a guard who only glanced inside and did not enter the cell to check.

Slocum closed the door and peered through the grating, confident enough of his handiwork to drop the locking bar back into place. The Institute guards were sloppy and there was no reason for them to doubt this was Peter Helmann in the cell. The other guards hunted for intruders in the tunnels.

As Slocum walked back to the temporary morgue, he wrestled with another problem. Peter Helmann would be carried out. How were he and Gretchen going to escape? He had considered hiding all three bodies and letting the grave diggers carry the trio of them out, but he was worried that they might actually check the contents when they found someone already had done their work for them.

"You boys're prompt. Can't wait to get them dead bodies in the ground, eh?" A guard said.

"Come on," Slocum said urgently. He laced up the canvas with quick movements whereas Gretchen had been working slowly, lovingly, as if she were actually burying her father in this shroud.

"Keep quiet, Papa," she said, bending to kiss him quickly before Slocum finished closing the canvas bag.

"We've got to get into the next cell. Let's hope the undertaker and his friends are moving slow this early in the morning."

"Morning?" Gretchen asked, as if it had not occurred to her. "I've lost all sense of time."

"Let's hope that's all you lose," Slocum said, pushing her ahead of him into a cell with an inmate cowering in the corner. The man began gibbering and drooling like a wild animal. Slocum put his finger to his lips to quiet the man, but it only made his cry out. Slocum considered other ways to silence him, then decided it hardly mattered. The inmates all put up a fuss whenever anyone came by. The guards were used to it. Even if the man got up and screamed that he had a man and a woman in the cell with him, Slocum doubted anyone would pay any heed.

"John," Gretchen said softly. "I know him."

"What?" He turned and looked at her, then followed down her arm and across her pointing index finger. She meant the lunatic. "What do you mean that you know him?"

"This is Old Man Evans. He disappeared a couple years ago and his . . ."

"Who took over his business?" Slocum asked, catching the drift of Gretchen's accusation.

"His son-in-law. Mr. Evans owns—owned—the mercantile. For Knipsen it did a good business."

"This is another score to settle," Slocum said. He saw how the man's eyes widened at the mention of his name. Or was it mention of his son-in-law?

"Settle it how?" asked Gretchen. "Sorry, I keep forgetting you're not from these parts. His son-in-law was killed in a robbery last year. His daughter disappeared and nobody knows what happened to her."

Slocum put it all together. Evans's son-in-law locked up his stumbling block to a thriving business. Either the daughter killed her husband or he died in an actual robbery, but the daughter lit out and nobody was left to champion Evans. It might not matter from the look of the man. He was emaciated and ill treated, and might have gone entirely insane, if he hadn't been when he was checked into the Breiland Institute for the Insane. This would have been Peter Helmann's fate if Gretchen hadn't enlisted his help.

Slocum cautioned her to silence when he heard the cell door next to them open. He wanted to peer out, but knew better than to rock the boat now. He heard men grunting, then: "Coulda been worse. Who'd you think already gift-wrapped 'em fer us, Micah?"

Micah answered. "Danged if I know. Surely wasn't His Highness Dr. Poston. He don't stir off his ass to even look at these stiffs. All he does is sign the death certify-cates."

"Got 'em here. Three death certificates, three bodies."

"Let's get to the cemetery. We can get back to town before lunch."

Slocum listened to one grave digger chide the other for being sweet on a window woman, and even make certain suggestions about how she came to be widowed. The clatter of wheels told Slocum they were moving the bodies out of the cell block. He heaved a sigh and looked at Gretchen.

"They're gone already," Slocum said, heaving a sigh. His plan had worked. Peter Helmann would be taken past the guards and nobody would be the wiser. "Now we have to get out of here ourselves and follow them to the cemetery."

Gretchen clutched Slocum's arm in warning.

"Dang it, they's gonna skin us alive if they see that," said the one Slocum had identified as Micah.

The locking bar dropped into place on their cell. Slocum swung around and began pounding on the door, shouting, "We're not inmates. Let us out! You make a mistake!"

"Only mistake made round here," Micah said, "is us not chargin' Dr. Poston 'nuff to bury you scum when you finally do ever'one a favor and croak!" With that touching sentiment, the grave digger hurried off, leaving Slocum and Gretchen in the cell with the old mercantile owner.

14

"Calm down," Slocum said sharply as Gretchen hammered her fists against the door. "We know how to get out. Let me see." He drew his knife and slid it between the door and jamb, moving it upward until he felt the blade pressing into the locking bar. He strained a little as he tried to lift the bar. Then he used both hands on the knife and finally dropped to the floor so he could put his entire weight and strength onto the hilt of the knife.

The bar didn't budge.

"Cotter pin," Evans said in a cracked voice. "They got cotter pins that secure the bar. Won't lift until the cotter pin's taken out."

"None of the other bars were locked like that," Slocum said, looking at the haggard old man.

"Guards don't care. Them grave diggers ain't guards. They do things different."

Slocum went cold inside. There was more than one way to get out of the cell. Whenever the guards came to feed Evans, he could force them back because he had a six-shooter and Gretchen still clutched the derringer he had given her. Even if the guards tried to feed Evans using the small slot at the bottom of the door, Slocum knew he could threaten even two or three guards to open the door. They could get out eventually—but Peter Helmann would be buried alive unless they got to the cemetery in time.

"You take me with you and I'll tell ya how to git outta the cell," Evans said.

"I promise," Slocum said. He looked squarely at the man to see if any cunning danced in those rheumy eyes. Evans had been in the Institute so long he might have become totally crazy, but Slocum saw nothing but infinite sadness mingled with hope at finally getting free.

"You'll die tryin' to git me out?" Evans said.

"I promise, too, Mr. Evans. You know me. Gretchen Helmann. My pa was wrongly locked up in here, just like you."

"That good-for-nuthin' boy of his done it, din't he?"

"Uwe did it," Gretchen said, bitterness in her tone. She lifted the derringer as if seeing it for the first time as the deadly weapon it was. "I can use this on Uwe. My own brother and I can kill him for what he's done!"

"You ain't lyin'." This wasn't a question. It was said with conviction.

"How do we get out if we can't pull the cotter pin from the locking bar?" asked Slocum.

"Back when I was stronger, I used a spoon to scrape at the wall. 'Bout got a block free when I wore out." Evans held out his hands. They shook like a leaf in a high wind. "Cain't hold nuthin' fer long anymore, either."

"Where?"

"That corner, down at the bottom," Evans said, pointing. "I dunno what I'da done if I got out. That came to me long after I stopped my diggin'."

"Here it is, John," Gretchen said excitedly. She brushed away dirt and filth to show that Evans had not been lying. "Let me use the knife, John."

"I'll do it," Slocum said, flopping onto his belly. He thrust out the knife and traced it around the block in the wall. The concrete crumbled away as he worked more and more frantically. Less than ten minutes of digging freed the block. Slocum swung around, kicked hard, and sent the block sailing out into the corridor, leaving a hole in the wall.

"I can't get through it," Slocum said, seeing how small the hole was. His wide shoulders wouldn't fit. He looked at Gretchen.

"I can do it. I'm much smaller."

"Lemme go," Evans said. "They done starved me to a cracker-ass thin son of a bitch. I been dreamin' of this."

"Do you have enough strength to pull the pin out and get the bar lifted?" asked Slocum. They'd be in a world of trouble if Evans got caught. Or if he collapsed.

"Try me. I can run on pure nerve fer a spell," Evans said. The decrepit old man began wiggling, got his shoulders through the opening easily, and then let Slocum push him out the same way he had the stone block.

"Do you think he can do it, John?"

"If not, you're next. Otherwise, we have to scrape out a couple more blocks."

"There's no rush," Gretchen said. "Other than me wanting to get out of here and . . ." Her blue eyes went wide when she realized what Slocum already had. "Oh, no. Papa!"

The door swung open. Evans supported himself with great effort, but he smiled from ear to ear. Most of his teeth were missing, but it was the sweetest smile Slocum had ever seen.

"Get back inside," Slocum said. "You rest up, and we'll be back for you."

"You promised."

"I never go back on my word," Slocum assured him.

"I'll be a'waitin' fer ya." Evans staggered back into the cell and collapsed. Slocum saw why Poston hadn't bothered chaining him. Evans was too weak to be a menace after all the years starved and locked up.

"How do we get out of the cell block?" asked Gretchen. "Shoot our way out?"

"You're too quick with that gun," Slocum said. He looked out into the guard area. His heart sank. Nobody was on duty now. How could he threaten men who weren't there?

"So? Back down the trapdoor?"

"Back down the trapdoor," he agreed. Slocum didn't like wandering around blindly in the dark, but saw no other way. Time pressed down on him like a giant rock. He doubted the grave diggers would be able to make very good time to the cemetery with the three bodies, but they had said they were anxious to return to town.

He yanked up the door and looked down into the tunnels. He swung around and hurried down the ladder, jumping the last few feet. Slocum caught Gretchen as she missed a rung and ended up in his arms.

"This isn't so bad," she said, giving him a quick kiss. "I only wish we had more time."

He put her down, got his bearings from where he thought the cell block overhead was in relation to the rest of the Institute, then started along the dark tunnel, letting the light from above guide him for a dozen paces. Then the faint light vanished entirely. He came to a branching corridor and took it, sure he was heading in the right direction. He had seen homing pigeons find their way home after being taken hundreds of miles from their coops. In a way, he had a similar sense of direction. All he needed were small hints.

And luck.

He looked straight up and saw the faint square of light above his head after blundering along for more than ten minutes.

"Another trapdoor?"

"It's not the one that opens into Poston's office, but it's close." Slocum used his last lucifer to find the ladder and scramble up the rungs. He pushed at the trapdoor. It opened easily into a storage room. Equipment was hung on hooks. He saw more than a dozen straightjackets piled on a table. Inmate smocks were baled like cotton, and unrecognizable metal gadgets were stacked along the walls.

"Help me up," Gretchen said, reaching the opening. Slocum grabbed her wrist and lifted her to the floor.

He opened the room door and immediately closed it.

"Bad news," he said. "We're in a room just off the lobby. Poston and Laramie are out there, and it doesn't look as if they plan to move any time soon."

"We have to go. We *have* to!"

Slocum considered shooting, and again discarded the notion. This place teemed with strong, well-armed guards. If Poston was back, that meant Jonah was around somewhere close. Slocum looked again and saw the two men going to Poston's office. The door wasn't closed all the way but stood ajar, giving Slocum and Gretchen the chance to hear anything going on outside.

"Are you up for a little acting?"

"Anything," Gretchen said. He hoped she wasn't simply saying that. He grabbed a straightjacket and handed it to her.

"Get into it. I'll lace it up."

"What?" Her outrage was evident on her lovely face. "I won't do any such thing!"

"Do it and we get out of here," he said. "Otherwise, your pa is going to be taking a dirt nap any time now."

"You—" Gretchen bit back her anger. She took the canvas jacket and began slipping it on. "You will owe me for this, John Slocum. You will!"

"Collect later. Right now, we need to get out of here." While she was clumsily putting on the straightjacket, Slocum found a guard's jacket and slipped it on. The cloth flapped around his body because it was many sizes too large. He might have found one of Jonah's spare outfits. This worked well for Slocum since it allowed him to keep on his six-shooter while hiding it.

"Ready?" he asked. Slocum spun her around when she didn't answer and began lacing up the straightjacket, fastening the arms behind her back. He had to cinch it up tight enough to look believable, but not so tight as to prevent her from escaping if anything happened to him.

"You'll pay for this," she muttered. Slocum grabbed a convenient strap and lifted her up, twisted her around so her face was away from Poston's office door, and then stepped into the corridor leading to the lobby.

"We have to go past Poston and Laramie," he said softly. "Don't yell too loud."

"You son of a bitch!" Gretchen shouted.

Slocum tensed, grabbed her, and bent her forward so her face was hidden. He saw what Gretchen already had. Coming toward them were two guards, both carrying bloodstained quirts. Slocum wrestled with her and slammed her into the wall as the two guards passed. He kept Gretchen away and tried to prevent them from seeing his face.

"Where's that one goin'?" asked the larger of the guards.

"Upstairs," Slocum said, struggling to keep Gretchen from bolting and running. She made the struggle look real. Slocum was sweating hard as he wrestled with her.

"To Ludmilla's?" The guard laughed. "She needs another whore. The last one upped and ran away from her." With this, the guard and his partner continued down the corridor toward the rooms where they beat the inmates. Slocum regretted not being able to deal with them and prevent some poor wight getting his face beat in, but Peter Helmann's predicament was more pressing.

"Clear to the door," whispered Gretchen. She tried to run, but her feet slid on the slick floor and she went to her knees. Slocum had to pull her along because she had fallen directly in front of Poston's door. A quick look inside showed the director arguing with Laramie.

Slocum got Gretchen to her feet and headed toward the front doors. They were almost there when the guard who had spoken came back, slapping the quirt against the palm of his left hand.

"You need help gettin' her upstairs?"

"No, I can handle her," Slocum said. He swung Gretchen around and aimed her up the stairs. He didn't have to tell her to cooperate so the guard would go back to his bloody chores.

"Is he still watching?" whispered Gretchen.

"Yeah," Slocum said. "We've got a guard coming down the hall on the second floor, too." He picked her up bodily and set her onto her feet. Leaning close, he said, "Go to him."

"You takin' that one up to Ludmilla?" The guard asked. He brightened when he saw Gretchen's face. "Hey, this is the one what escaped. You're gonna get a big bonus, maybe a roll in the sack with her."

Gretchen lowered her head and charged, driving a shoulder into the man. Slocum moved as fast, coming alongside. He fumbled a little pushing aside the bulky jacket; then everything went smoothly. His Colt Navy came out and landed alongside the man's head. The guard sank to the floor, out like a light.

"Get me *out*," Gretchen said, thrashing about.

"Hold still," Slocum said. He unlaced the arms and let her skin out of the straightjacket. "Get him in it. We can dump him in one of the rooms." Slocum held his six-shooter and glanced up toward Ludmilla's domain, then down to the lobby. He feared the commotion would bring the two guards or worse, Poston and Laramie.

"It's harder getting him into this thing than I thought," Gretchen grumbled.

"Almost as hard as undressing a woman." Slocum was rewarded with a glare that melted like snow on a spring day. Gretchen actually laughed.

"You don't need to worry your head about that," she told him. "Next time, I'll help."

Slocum and Gretchen dragged the unconscious guard into the nearest room, dumped him, and closed the door. They again faced the flight of stairs to the lobby.

"Walk like you are supposed to be here," Slocum said. He moved to shield Gretchen from sight if Poston might glance out of his office, but the director and the outlaw were still arguing, more heatedly than before, and never saw them. Slocum and Gretchen reached the front doors and were through them in a flash.

Gretchen heaved a sigh, but Slocum knew they were far from getting away. They had to return to where the horse was tethered and then find the cemetery.

"Anyone in sight?" Slocum asked. He squinted as he stepped out to study the turret where he had first seen the sniper. No one was there. He checked the bell tower. Empty. Slocum heaved a sigh of relief. A sentry in either of those elevated watchtowers would have spotted them in an instant.

"Front gate?" suggested Gretchen.

"Stick close to the building until I can see where I came over the wall," Slocum said. "Then we run for it."

He kept an eye peeled for Gold Tooth, but the guard wasn't on patrol. Slocum got a tad uneasy at not finding patrols on the grounds. Before, he couldn't step out of the Institute without stumbling over a couple. Now, he almost wished that were true so he could feel better about what had to be done. Slocum forced himself not to pull out his pocket watch and see how much time had elapsed since Peter Helmann had been taken from his cell. This would only spook Gretchen, and wouldn't do a damn thing to speed up the man's rescue.

"See anyone?"

"Nobody," Gretchen assured him. "Do we walk like we're supposed to be here?"

"We run like our tails're on fire," Slocum said. He threw caution to the wind and ran as hard as he could for the wall. He got there only seconds before Gretchen. He bent, took her boot in his cupped hands, and heaved hard. She flew upward and caught the edge of the wall. Grunting, she pulled herself over, then cursed.

"Got caught on the barbed wire," she called.

Slocum took a step back, then launched himself up the wall. His fingers caught at the crumbling edge of the masonry. For a moment he thought he was going to fall, but Gretchen grabbed his left wrist in both her hands and tugged. He kept scrambling, and quickly flopped belly-down over the top of the wall, kicked, and plunged to the far side. He landed hard but recovered fast.

"Jump," he called. Gretchen didn't hesitate. He found his arms full of woman in an instant. Staggering, he fought to keep his balance. With a deft turn, he deposited her feet to the ground and righted her. "Run again," he told her. They found his horse and mounted it and Gretchen mounted one right beside it.

"What's wrong?" Gretchen asked when Slocum simply sat astride his horse.

"I don't know where we're heading," he admitted. "Where's the cemetery?"

"Oh," she said in a small voice. "There are two."

"Which one's a potter's field?"

"This way!" Gretchen wheeled her horse around and galloped off. Slocum wanted to warn her not to exhaust her horse too soon, but he knew what drove her. He couldn't imagine what being buried alive would be like. A shudder passed through him when he remembered some friends who had insisted on a bell attached to a rope that went into their coffins when they died. If they were accidentally buried alive, they would be able to let the groundskeeper know by pulling the bell rope.

If there even was a groundskeeper where he was headed, Peter Helmann would not have such an elaborate warning system.

"How far?" Slocum called to the woman who still rode ahead of him.

"A couple miles."

"Slow down. You'll kill your horse. We have to get there

fast, and that's not going to happen if we have to walk the last mile."

Gretchen reluctantly slowed her horse to a trot. Slocum came even with her.

"We'll get there in time," he told her.

"I hope so." She turned her stricken face toward him. "There wasn't any other way to get him out, was there?"

"Not without a lot of killing."

"I wouldn't have cared. I'd have helped."

"We didn't have the firepower," he assured her. She nodded again and looked straight ahead along the narrow road. Tears ran down her cheeks, but Gretchen said nothing more.

Slocum took the time to check the road, and found evidence that a heavy wagon had passed by recently. A mud puddle showed tracks about the right size for a wagon used as a hearse, and piles of horse shit were still fresh and just drawing flies.

"They're not more than a half hour ahead of us."

"If only we hadn't taken so long getting out of that horrid place," Gretchen said.

"There!" Slocum called, pointing. "There's the entrance to the cemetery." He urged his tired horse onward. Gretchen followed, her horse beginning to falter from exhaustion. They had galloped more than two miles before breaking stride and allowing the horses to take a slower gait.

"Where are the grave diggers? I don't see them anywhere. John, we came to the wrong cemetery!"

"No, we didn't," he told her. He was positive they had followed the tracks of the grave diggers' wagon, even if the men were nowhere to be seen.

Slocum let out a low groan when he saw what confronted them. The grave diggers were gone, probably back to Knipsen to tend to their urgent business. He hadn't expected them to have the three graves already dug—but they had.

They had come into the graveyard and put their three bodies into graves. It had taken them only a few minutes to replace the dirt.

Slocum stared aghast at three fresh graves with dirt mounded above them.

"Which one's my papa's?" Gretchen asked in a choked voice.

Slocum didn't know.

15

"They buried him alive!"

Slocum stared at the three graves. Peter Helmann was in one of them. But which one?

"The grave diggers," Gretchen said, her blue eyes wild as she looked around frantically. "Where are they?"

"On their way back to Knipsen," Slocum said. He had to force himself to stay calm. If he panicked now, Peter Helmann was a goner. But his mind went blank when he stared down at the three new graves. Helmann could be in any of them. Or was there some small fact Slocum was overlooking that would get the man out of his early grave faster than digging at random?

"Where are you going?" Slocum saw Gretchen mount her horse and saw at the reins to turn the pony's head toward town.

"The grave diggers. They have to be stopped."

"Why?" Slocum spoke to thin air. Gretchen whipped her horse into a gallop that died before she reached the edge of the cemetery. The horse had been pushed past its endurance, but Gretchen continued to whip at it. The horse dutifully stumbled on.

Slocum looked again at the graves, then knew what he

had to do. He swung into the saddle and went after Gretchen. He overtook her before she had gone another hundred yards down the road.

Reaching over, he grabbed her around the waist and swung her from her horse. Hanging onto the shrieking woman, he reined in and slowed. Gretchen's horse stopped almost immediately, tuckered out from the new exertion.

"Let me go, damn you! I have to get the grave diggers. I have to make them tell me which grave my father's in!"

Slocum dropped her to the ground. She lost her balance and went to hands and knees. In this position, she hung her head, crying openly.

"Why'd you stop me? Do you want to kill my papa?"

"Think, dammit," Slocum raged. "The grave diggers thought they were burying dead men. They wouldn't know which grave they put your pa in. How could they, unless they opened each shroud?"

"They might have. I've heard tell of them robbing corpses."

"Think, Gretchen, think. They picked up the bodies from the Breiland Institute. How many bodies from there would have anything of value on them?"

"What are we going to do?"

"We've both got to dig. I think I know which one to start on."

"How?"

Slocum reached down, took her hand, and swung her into the saddle behind him. Her arms circled his waist naturally, but he felt her quaking with emotion.

"We dig on the middle grave," he said. "We ride around the cemetery first and hunt for shovels that might have been left, then we dig in the middle grave."

"Why that one?"

"I sandwiched your pa between the other two corpses to hide any movement he might make. He would have been piled onto their cart second. He would have been loaded into their wagon second. Let's hope he was buried second."

Slocum trotted about the graveyard and found a rusty shovel with a broken handle. Gretchen jumped down and grabbed it as if it would save her life—and it might save her pa's. Slocum didn't see any other digging implements anywhere. He rode back to the three graves after a final circuit of the cemetery and found Gretchen digging like a gopher, dirt flying all over as she scraped away the top layer over the grave.

Slocum jumped down and added his own effort, using his broad-bladed knife. What seemed an eternity was only a few minutes. The dirt was still soft and the grave diggers hadn't bothered putting stones on the grave to keep away coyotes. Slocum hoped that didn't mean they had buried Peter Helmann a full six feet. From what he had overheard when he had eavesdropped on Micah and his partner, they weren't likely to put themselves out. They had complained at the measly ten dollars a corpse they received from the county. This gave Slocum some small conviction that they had not dug deeply or placed the bodies well.

"Wait, John, look. The canvas bag!" Gretchen threw aside her broken shovel and began pulling away the dirt with her hands. They had dug down only three feet, about what Slocum had anticipated.

"Let me," Slocum said. He brushed away some of the dirt and used his knife on the laces he had fastened. The knife blade had become dull and nicked, but it still severed the rope. He pulled the canvas flaps apart. For a moment, he didn't understand what he looked at. Then his belly flopped.

They had found Peter Helmann's grave, but the man was turned over onto his belly in the grave. He had fought and died.

Then Slocum let out a cry of surprise when Helmann rolled onto his back and looked up. The man squinted at the bright light.

"Gretchen?" he said in a hoarse croaking voice.

"Yes, Papa, yes! It's me. Me and John Slocum."

"You promised. You kept that promise."

"Let me get you out of there," Slocum said, moving dirt away as fast as he could so Peter Helmann could sit up in his grave. The man was filthy but alive. His chains rattled as he reached up so Gretchen could help him stand.

The effort was noble, but the flesh was weak. Both of them collapsed in a pile. Slocum helped Gretchen to her feet, and then they both dragged Helmann from the grave. The hot sun beat down on them. Slocum shaded Helmann the best he could as they moved toward a lone mesquite at the edge of the cemetery. It wouldn't provide much in the way of protection from the burning-hot Texas sun, but was better than staying in the direct rays.

"Get the canteen off my saddle," Slocum told Gretchen. She hesitated, then went to obey.

"How'd you survive in the grave?" Slocum asked. He hadn't wanted to ask the question while Gretchen was listening.

"Rolled onto my belly," Helmann croaked out. "Arched my back. When the dirt came crashing down I'd trapped a bit of air under me. Sorta leaked out through the lacing until, the dirt clogged it. Then all I could do was wait for you."

Peter Helmann looked hard at Slocum, then smiled. "I surely am glad you're not my son."

Slocum's eyebrows shot up. "Why's that?"

"The little bastard'd have let me die."

"Here, Papa, you drink slow now so you won't choke."

"Just like her ma," Peter Helmann said, grinning through chapped lips at Gretchen. He gingerly sipped at the water, most of it spilling from his mouth and washing his chin clean. Slocum knew they'd have to find a stream to get more water, but that could wait a while.

"Taste good, Papa?"

"Sweeter than any *liebfraumilch*," Helmann said. He spoke rapidly to his daughter in German. She glanced at Slocum, blushed, and looked away. Helmann laughed.

"What's going on?" Slocum asked.

"She likes you," Peter Helmann said. "That's all right. I do, too. Anyone who rescues me from that hellhole is all right in my book." He held up his shackled hands. "What can you do about these?"

Slocum said, "While Gretchen's fixing some grub, I'll see what I can do."

"I don't—" she protested.

"You do," Helmann said sharply. "I haven't had any food in days. Or it seems like it. That slop they called food was worse than what I'd give to the hogs."

Gretchen calmed down and went to see what was in the saddlebags.

"She's headstrong, Gretchen is, but a strong man can tame her."

"Let me see your wrists," Slocum said. The man was hardly out of his grave and was trying to play matchmaker.

Examining the locks closely, Slocum finally decided on the best way of prying the locks open. A smithy's hammer and chisel would have been best, but there were more ways to open a lock than brute strength. Using his knife, Slocum whittled a bit of wood from the mesquite bush, then scraped the side of one shackle with the knife and got a thin sliver of metal. He worked the metal in with the wood, then began fishing around inside the lock with his crude lockpick.

Before Gretchen had finished cobbling together a meal of salt-back pork and some beans, he had opened one lock. Peter Helmann's wrist was chaffed raw from the metal. Gretchen fed her father while Slocum worked on the other wrist. It took more skill to open this lock than the other, but he succeeded by the time Helmann was finished eating.

"Where'd you learn that? Did you apprentice as a lock-smith?"

"I prefer the open range to a shop," Slocum said in way of answer. He had spent more than a fair share of his time with shackles of his own on wrists and ankles and had worked himself free of a few in his day.

"John's very talented," Gretchen said.

"In many ways, *liebchen*? You know this how?" Peter Helmann teased Gretchen, but she blushed furiously and began putting up the food.

"Not so fast," Slocum said to her. "I haven't eaten in a spell. Neither have you. Fix enough for both of us."

"It's all gone," she said. "There're cans of peaches and tomatoes."

"You pick one, I'll take the other," Slocum said. He rocked back and sat heavily looking at his handiwork. "There. The chains are off."

"I want to keep them," Peter Helmann said, staring at the opened locks and lengths of chain. "I want to never forget. I will put them over my fireplace and look at them every day."

"What are we going to do, Papa?" Gretchen looked forlorn. She handed Slocum a can of tomatoes. He took it, used his knife to open the top, and returned it to her. She gave him the peaches and began eating the tomatoes. Slocum saw the matter of who ate what had been decided for him. He didn't care. Peaches were good. Anything was, considering how long it had been since he had eaten his last meal back in the Knipsen restaurant.

"We are going to the Circle H and take it back!"

Slocum looked up from his peaches. He had done all he had promised Gretchen he would do. Now he had a score to settle with Laramie and Kinsley. Carbuncle had already paid, but Slocum wanted more. Other than Laramie and Kinsley with bullets in their double-crossing hearts, he wanted the money from the Austin bank robbery. It was his due, and it gave him a measure of revenge on Wilson for bilking him of his money the way he had.

Slocum turned a little harder when he thought of Poston and the entire staff of the Breiland Institute for the Insane. That Institute had to be closed down once and for all.

He had promised Old Man Evans he would get him out,

too. So many promises, and each was as needful of fulfilling as the next.

"I'll see you back to your ranch house," Slocum said. "I'll need some supplies."

"For the trail?" Gretchen asked. The apprehension in her eyes told him it was time to move on. She was looking to him to solve all her problems, and he was hardly able to see to his own.

"Men inside the Institute owe me," he said.

"He is a good man," said Helmann. "He can ride on, if he chooses. You will see me to the ranch?"

"You can ride Gretchen's horse. Mine's stronger and can carry both Gretchen and me." Slocum saw Peter Helmann nod slowly. Then the man smiled crookedly.

"Is there room in your saddlebags for these?" He held up the chains Poston had put on him.

"You weren't joshing about hanging them over your fireplace, were you?" Slocum shook his head. It made no sense to him to be reminded of the bad times. Those crowded into his nightmares too often, but he knew other men were different.

He took the chains and found room for them where his food had ridden.

"Mount up," Slocum called. "You need help?"

"I can make it," Peter Helmann said. "Being free gives me strength. That and the food."

Slocum mounted, then reached down and pulled Gretchen behind him. This time she rode with her arms around his waist, but something had changed. She was stiffer than before when she had been frightened for her father's well-being. He knew why. He had let her know that he wasn't going to be lassoed and had business to tend to. Telling Gretchen or her father what that business was would only put them in danger.

The Texas Ranger wasn't going to quit looking for the bank robbers until they were all dead or had run far enough to be out of his jurisdiction.

Slocum wanted to be across the Rio Grande, in Mexico, spending the money before Ranger Coldcreek knew he was gone.

"You don't have to drift on, John," Gretchen said, her breath warm in his ear. "I can make it worth your while staying."

"You and your pa have a powerful lot of trouble ahead," Slocum said, remembering his brief stay in the Circle H bunkhouse. "Your brother's got friends among the hired hands."

"You mean Billy? He's a snake," Gretchen said hotly. "There are a couple more, but if we take care of Uwe and Billy, the others will go along with anything Pa says. They follow money and aren't loyal to anybody."

"A crew worth firing," Slocum said. He had worked as both a cowboy and a trail master for cattle ranches from Texas all the way north to Montana. It was never a good idea to have men working for you who thought only of money.

"You sound as if you have experience. When Billy's fired, we'll need a good foreman."

"He said he was ramrod, not foreman. That means he's going to be taking a herd out soon."

"What! Uwe must have sold the cattle! He can't do that. He—" Gretchen began sputtering incoherently.

Peter Helmann rode over, and Gretchen calmed enough to tell him what she suspected her brother was doing. The two of them spent the next ten minutes ignoring Slocum and talking in guttural German. To Slocum it sounded like two cats fighting. He knew they had plenty to talk over, and he didn't mind being dealt out of the hand. Slocum thought hard as he rode in the direction Gretchen had aimed him.

As twilight settled on the Hill Country, Slocum saw a neatly lettered sign proclaiming this to be Circle H land. He considered getting off the road and approaching the ranch house from a different direction. He doubted Uwe Helmann had any idea his father and sister were paying him an unexpected visit, but lead would fly when he found out. They had to take him unawares or men would die.

Slocum wasn't averse to swapping lead, especially with Billy after the ramrod had tried to murder him in his sleep, but an all-out range war wasn't going to solve Peter Helmann's problems.

Take out his son, take out Billy, and Helmann would be back in control of the ranch.

"You shouldn't ride straight in," Slocum said when he saw that Peter Helmann was going to do just that. "Creep up, get an idea what's going on, then decide what you should do."

"A good idea," Helmann said. "I would thrash my own son, but I am still weak. I must recover more."

Gretchen started to argue, then subsided.

Slocum led the way, circling the ranch house and coming up from behind the barn just a little after sundown. The cowboys were all chowing down from the sounds coming from the direction of the bunkhouse. But that didn't tell Slocum where to find Billy—and he had never laid eyes on Uwe Helmann.

"There!" cried Peter Helmann. "There he is. My son!"

Gretchen jumped to the ground and fumbled for the rifle sheathed at Slocum's knee. He grabbed her arm and held her. Their eyes locked.

"This isn't your fight," he said.

"It is, too! He's my brother."

Slocum looked at Peter Helmann, who had dismounted. The man balled his fists. In the darkness, Slocum heard the knuckles popping as Helmann tensed and relaxed his hands.

"It's *his* fight," Slocum said. Gretchen saw her father marching from the side of the barn directly toward Uwe. She sagged. She knew Slocum was right.

16

Slocum tried to see what was going on, but Uwe Helmann had kept walking away from his father, probably never seeing him. The darkness convinced Slocum to act, in spite of what he had said about this being between father and son. He put his heels to his horse and walked forward. As he went, his hand rested on the butt of his Colt Navy.

"Where'd he go?" Slocum called to Peter Helmann. The man turned slowly, glared at Slocum, then disappeared into the same shadows that had swallowed his son. Sliding his leg over his saddle, Slocum dropped to the ground. He drew his six-shooter and advanced slowly. Something warned him this wasn't going as any of them had expected.

Gretchen ran up behind him.

"What is it, John?"

"Stay back," he said. Slocum turned, his six-gun cocked and aimed at the sound of horses galloping off. He rushed forward and came up beside Peter Helmann. The man shook his fist in the air at the retreating horsemen.

"It was Uwe and that good-for-nothing friend of his."

"Billy?"

"Him," Peter Helmann said angrily. "I couldn't get to

them in time. They rode off. How dare they? Come back here!" Helmann called, but his voice was cracked and weak. Slocum heard him fine, but nobody more than a few yards away would have noticed.

"It might be for the best," Slocum said. "Rest up. You'll be more effective when he gets back if you've slept in your own bed and eaten at your own table after being in the Institute for so long."

"I wanted this out with him now. Fetch a horse, Slocum. I'm going after him."

"Papa, no, John is right."

"You might go to the bunkhouse and see who's there," Slocum suggested. "Uwe might not be the choice of many of the cowboys to lead them. A few allies at your back can go a long way."

"None of them like Billy," Gretchen said. Slocum heard something more in her voice whenever she mentioned the ramrod. "Go on into the house, Papa. Do as John says. It's the smart thing to do."

"Bring the chains from your saddlebags," Peter Helmann said. His anger didn't fade as much as it changed from heat to smolder.

Slocum pulled the heavy chains from the saddlebags. His horse whinnied in relief at being freed of this extra weight. Slocum carried them into the ranch house, and stopped when he saw Peter Helmann standing in the middle of the sitting room. The man was crying openly. Slocum felt a little uneasy at the sight, but he understood. He waited a few seconds, then cleared his throat.

"Where do you want these?" he asked, rattling the chains. This gave Helmann the chance to wipe away the tears and face Slocum with a set jaw and determination.

"There, on the mantel," the man said.

Slocum heard movement behind him. He dropped into a crouch, drew, and aimed his six-shooter at the cowboy he had met the first time he had been at the ranch. The cowboy's hands went high and his eyes opened wide. He saw

Slocum and the threat he posed, but he was looking at Peter Helmann.

"You got back," the cowboy said.

"We have some talkin' to do, Lyle," said the owner of the Circle H.

"They tole us you was crazy," Lyle said, his voice almost cracking with strain. "You ain't dangerous no more, are you, Mr. Helmann?"

"I'm damned dangerous, Lyle, but only to that worthless turd that put me in the asylum."

"You're talkin' 'bout your own son," the cowboy said uneasily.

"He's not my son. No longer. The only offspring I have is my daughter. Gretchen risked her life to get me out of that viper pit where Uwe put me."

"You ain't crazy?" Lyle didn't sound convinced.

"He's no crazier than you are," Slocum said, relaxing. He thrust his six-gun back into its holster. "Or are you loco enough to think there's anything wrong with Mr. Helmann?"

"We was told," Lyle began. He swallowed hard. "Sorry. I don't know what to think."

"Then I'll tell you," Helmann said. "I want Uwe hogtied and brought to me if any of the hands see him. I don't want him killed." What ought to have been a comforting request—not wanting his son murdered—turned more chilling because of the way Peter Helmann spoke. The rancher wanted his son alive so he could endure the same torture he had inflicted on his father.

"You can do as you please to Billy," said Gretchen.

"You mean that?" Lyle looked from Peter Helmann to his daughter and back. "Really, after you and him—"

"That's enough, Lyle," Gretchen snapped. She glared at the cowboy, but Slocum now realized what sparked Gretchen's rage every time she mentioned Billy. It was easy to see why Billy would have a lech for a lovely blond woman like Gretchen, but what had she seen in Billy?

Somewhere along the way, he had thrown in with Uwe and dumped her, probably because the ramrod saw the chance for money he would never get by cozying up to Gretchen.

"Who's the foreman?" Slocum asked.

"Well, all we got right now's Billy and he—"

"You think Lyle here would make a good foreman?" Slocum asked Helmann, cutting off the cowboy's long-winded explanations. The question shut Lyle up and made Gretchen glower at Slocum.

"I don't see why not. You up for it, son?" Peter Helmann asked of the cowboy.

"I reckon I kin do 'bout anything," Lyle said. "Reckon I've been doin' most everything since Billy got all uppity. He let most chores go by the wayside."

"You're foreman of the Circle H," Helmann said. "Get together your top hands and bring them back here. We're going to have a meeting and get the ranch operating again."

"And what 'bout Uwe and Billy?"

A dark cloud came over Peter Helmann as he said, "I told you what I expected. I'll let all the men know when you get 'em in here."

"Yes, sir, right away, Mr. Helmann," Lyle said. He tipped his hat in Gretchen's direction, then lit out for the bunkhouse to round up the top hands for the meeting.

"I don't want to sit around and listen to all that you're going to say about Uwe, Billy, and running the Circle H," Gretchen said.

"It's been a hard, trying time for all of us. You run along, Gretchen. And thank you for springing me from that prison."

"Oh, Papa," Gretchen said, going to him and kissing him on the cheek. "I'd do anything for you."

"I'll be moseying on, too," Slocum said to no one in particular since the two of them were again talking in rapid-fire German. He slipped out the door as Lyle and a half-dozen cowboys came up the steps.

"Thank you, Slocum," Lyle said. "When I fetched you

that grub a while back, I never thought it'd win me a job like foreman of the Circle H."

"Don't let him down," Slocum said. "He's been chewed up and spit out. He deserves better."

"Yes, sirree, I agree with that. Come on in, boys. We got some palaverin' to do." Lyle herded the men into the ranch house, leaving Slocum alone on the porch.

The humid summer breeze did nothing to erase the sweat on Slocum's forehead. He stepped down and looked toward a wooded area some distance off where lightning bugs flitted about, glowing madly and then vanishing into the darkness. Slocum felt a kinship with those fireflies. He had blazed bright for a spell. Now it was time for him to fade into the darkness. He had more than one score to settle, and it was high time he started.

Walking toward the barn where he had left his horse, he heard steps behind him. He turned, hand going for his six-shooter. When he saw Gretchen's distinctive outline against the light pouring from the front of the ranch house, he relaxed.

"You were going to ride off without so much as a good-bye?"

"I'd have been back by," he said.

"Liar," Gretchen spit. "You were leaving. I know it."

Slocum wasn't going to argue. He had more than the woman on his mind right now. How long it would take Ranger Coldcreek to find him was anyone's guess.

"You don't want me around any longer than necessary," he told her.

"Because the law's after you? I figured that from the start. All that cut-up newspaper from the *Houston Tri-weekly Gazette* meant you got double-crossed, didn't it? From the way you talked about Laramie, he was the leader who did it."

"Don't go getting too smart," Slocum warned, "or you'll find yourself in trouble up to your pretty little neck. I doubt that Texas Ranger would hesitate to throw even a

lovely woman like you in jail, if he thought she knew anything about a bank robbery."

"You think I'm pretty?"

The question took Slocum aback.

"And you worry about getting me involved with the law.
That's sweet."

"That's not something many women have ever said
about me. Hardly any," Slocum said. Then he laughed
harshly. "None, if you want an exact number."

"You weren't sweet back at the brothel, when Ludmilla
was watching. You were . . . hard." Gretchen moved closer.
She threw her arms around Slocum's neck and pulled his
face to hers for a big, wet kiss.

When Slocum broke off, he said, "You were tied up.
You couldn't do anything but go along with what was necessary. If we hadn't done what we did, Ludmilla would
have killed us both. We were locked up in that room."

"We were," Gretchen said softly. "And I was tied up. I
couldn't do much more than struggle. It was good. I liked
it. A lot." She pressed closer to him, her firm breasts rubbing against his chest. She caught his hand and pulled it
down to those breasts, then stepped away so she could
guide his hand even lower. She released it so she could
press her own hand into his crotch. "I liked feeling you
there. Did you like it? Was I as good as the other women
you've had?"

"Better," Slocum said, not sure if he was lying.

"Because I enjoyed it so much?"

"Yes," he said. He kissed her again. She flowed into his
arms as if their bodies were molded together. Gretchen
pressed hard against him, lifted one leg, and tried to curl it
around his waist. Her skirts got in the way. He reached
down, ran his hand along her sleek, smooth flesh and up to
her thigh, carrying her skirt with him as he went.

She hopped a little and got her leg curled around him
when her skirt was rolled around her waist.

"I'm still not wearing bloomers," she whispered in his

ear. Then she began to lick at his earlobe. When her hot, wet tongue probed into the ear channel, Slocum caught his breath. He was responding powerfully to her.

"Is being tied up the only way you get off?"

"I don't know," Gretchen said. "What did you have in mind?"

"Getting out of plain sight, for starters," Slocum said.

"It's exciting, thinking somebody might come out and see what we're doing," Gretchen said.

"Not if it's your pa and not if he has a shotgun."

"He likes you. You saved him. He wouldn't say anything about me giving you a little reward for what you've done for us."

"Is that what you two were talking about on the way back here?" Slocum asked.

"You'll have to convince me I should tell you. What do you have in mind to do that's convincing? Does it have anything to do with this?" She reached down to his crotch and pressed her palm into the bulge there.

"Might be, it doesn't matter," Slocum said.

"It does, it does!" Gretchen turned almost frantic, then realized he was teasing her. "Oh, you!" She dropped her leg and stepped away. Her skirt fell back to a chaste level. As she turned, Slocum caught her around the waist and spun her around, taking her off her feet.

"Waaa!" she cried. "What are you doing?"

"Taking you to the woodshed," Slocum said. Gretchen squealed and struggled, but Slocum's grip was secure around her waist. He kicked open the barn door, then closed it behind them as he looked around the dark interior.

He took a few steps into the barn, then dropped her so she sprawled belly-down over a bale of hay. Gretchen started to push back up and turn, but Slocum put his hand in the middle of her back and held her down.

"No," he said. "Don't go getting all high-and-mighty on me."

"I want *you* all high-and-mighty. Like what I was feeling back in the yard," she said. Her breath came faster as she looked over her shoulder while Slocum unbuttoned the fly on his jeans and let his firm, steely shaft leap out. A ray of light caught it. Gretchen swallowed hard at the sight.

"You're talking too much," Slocum said, hiking her skirt and exposing her bare buttocks. He landed an open-handed swat on one firm, round cheek. She yelped as much in surprise as from the swat.

"I promise to be better."

"You're talking again," Slocum said, landing another swat on the other buttock. Gretchen settled down over the hay bale, her knees on the ground and her pert rear end up high for Slocum's attention. He spanked her a few more times, then knew he was not going to be able to continue, as much as Gretchen wanted. He felt as if he had sprouted a stick of dynamite from his groin and it was going to blow up at any instant.

Slocum dropped down behind her, running his hands over her warmed flesh. Gretchen shivered with need as he ran his fingers between her thighs and gently spread them, exposing the target they both wanted hit.

"Oh, yes, John, now, do it now. I'm so hot inside." Gretchen hesitated a moment, then said, "You're not going to spank me anymore because I spoke, will you?"

There was a plaintive quality to her question, but Slocum wasn't going to play around any longer. He couldn't. He ached so much it felt like he was going to go crazy from it.

He put his hands on either side of her on the hay bale and leaned forward, his hips moving forward so his long shaft parted her fleshy half-moons. She sighed as he probed further. He touched the gently scalloped nether lips with the tip of his manhood, and then paused. Heat boiled out from her interior. He felt the dampness seeping all around his shaft. And then he slipped forward in a smooth entry that caused them both to cry out in stark passion.

Surrounded by her clinging hot female flesh, he arched

his back and tried to drive himself even deeper. She squeezed down around him, as if a velvet glove had seized his organ in a vise-tight grip. Slocum stroked over Gretchen's flanks, feeling the outsides of her trembling thighs, moving lower to her calves.

Bending forward, he reached around under her, slipping his hand between her breasts and the hay in the bale. He clutched down firmly, released, and repeated this until Gretchen was sobbing in joy. He began rotating his hips and working himself ever deeper into her from behind. Gretchen lifted off the ground slightly and drove herself back into the circle of his groin. They fit together like a key in a lock—and together they unleashed a torrent of desire.

Gretchen gasped and threw back her head like a frisky pony. Slocum had to hang onto her waist to keep from slipping free. He rode her hard, driving in and out with increasing speed as her passions were being vented. As she settled down, he began a smoother, deeper penetration that caused friction to burn the entire length of his hidden manhood.

This sparked a new earthquake in Gretchen's trim young body that couldn't be contained. She cried out as he sank balls-deep into her from behind, then exploded within her clutching depths.

All too soon, the heat passed and Slocum eased back from her. The light that had spotlighted him earlier now cast a thin sliver across her bare buttocks. He didn't swat her again. This time he stroked gently, enjoying the flow of her skin under his callused fingers.

"Don't stop," she said.

"Too late for that," he said, laughing.

"Want me to see if there's anything I can do to . . . encourage you?"

Slocum swung around and sat on the bale, legs spread wide.

"Give it a try," Slocum said. "You never know what might come up."

Gretchen laughed and applied her mouth to the flaccid length between his thighs.

Then she pulled back in surprise and looked around when the barn door was yanked open.

17

"What the hell's goin' on?" The man standing in the barn door took a step inside. "I'll be switched. You two been goin' at it like dogs in heat!"

Slocum rolled to one side, pushing Gretchen to the other. He worked to get his pants up and find where he had dropped his gun belt. The last man in the world he had expected to be there right now was the Circle H ramrod. Billy stood leering, his thumbs stuck in his gun belt.

Slocum intended to put an end to the leering, once and for all.

"Don't reach for that hogleg, mister," Billy said. "Who the hell are you?" Billy stepped closer, then gasped. "Gretchen!"

"You son of a bitch!" the woman raged. She threw a handful of shoeing nails at him, causing him to duck. But as he flinched away from the nails, he also went for his six-shooter.

Slocum still hadn't pulled on his pants, but he found his Colt Navy. He drew the pistol, but it wasn't sitting comfortably in his hand when he fanned off two quick shots. The fanning action and his poor grip caused him to fumble. Both shots went wide.

Then Billy got the range. His first bullet tore past Slocum's ear. The second carved a groove in Slocum's forehead, just above his left eye. The head wound bled profusely and blood dripped down into Slocum's eyes from his eyebrow. The world went partly black as he was blinded in one eye. Squinting, depth perception gone, Slocum steadied his six-gun and got to his knees, waiting. He worked more by sound than sight.

He fired as something scraped across the barn floor. The instant his finger pulled the trigger, he knew he had been decoyed. Billy was trying to get him to exhaust his ammo. Slocum had three rounds left, but his attention was pulled in different directions. He used his shirt sleeve to mop at the head wound, tried to pull up his pants, and worried that Gretchen would get in the line of fire.

Too many things worked against him. He heard the barn door slam shut. Slocum stood, hitched up his pants, and then aimed, thinking Billy was decoying him again.

"He left, John," Gretchen said from behind him. "The yellow-belly ran!"

"Stay back," Slocum snapped. He put his pistol down for a moment while he dealt with his pants. He secured them around his middle, but the head wound oozed again. What sight he had regained in his eye disappeared again. He snatched up his six-shooter and went to the door, peered out one-eyed, and saw a dark figure running hard toward the back of the ranch house. Slocum raised his pistol to shoot, then stopped. He couldn't tell who he was shooting at.

In the dark, he might kill Peter Helmann or one of his cowboys by mistake.

He knew he should have fired when he heard Billy call, "Get the hell out of here! It's that Slocum I tried to kill! He's back! And that was Gretchen with him in the barn!"

From shadow came a mounted man. Slocum swiped the blood off his eyebrow and blinked hard. That must be Uwe Helmann. Earlier, he had ridden out before he'd seen his

father. Now he was being warned about what was going on
at the Circle H.

Slocum fired this time, but his impaired sight, the darkness, and the distance all worked against him. By the time
his hammer fell on an empty chamber, both Billy and Uwe
had ridden off.

"John, you let them get away!" Gretchen busily tried to
settle her skirt and didn't quite manage. It was still hiked
up, exposing her pert rear end. Slocum wiped away more
blood, then began reloading.

"John!" Gretchen spun on him. "What are you going to
do about Billy? About Uwe?"

Slocum turned a cold stare on the woman. She quailed
under his green eyes.

"I'll get them," Slocum said. "And you should pull
down your skirt before your butt gets too cold out in the
nighttime."

"What? Why, oh!" Gretchen reached behind and tugged
at the skirt until it dropped. She let out a sigh of relief at
getting decent as her father, Lyle, and the cowboys came
from inside the house.

Slocum noticed none of them had been in much of a
hurry to see what the shooting was all about.

"Why'd you shoot like that, Slocum?" asked Lyle, seeing that he was finishing reloading his six-shooter.

"Billy and your son came back," Slocum said, ignoring
the foreman and talking directly to Peter Helmann.

"Saddle up, boys. We can run 'em into the ground!"

Slocum saw that Helmann's order fell on deaf ears. The
men of the Circle H might be good cowboys, but they
lacked spine when it came to gunplay.

"I have a score to settle with Billy," Slocum said. "He
tried to murder me when I was here before."

"You mean that varmint tried to dry-gulch you?" Lyle
shook his head. Slocum wondered if the cowboy was truly
bewildered or if he had known and was now trying to make
it seem that he was innocent. Considering his cowardice in

not wanting to get on Uwe Helmann's trail, Lyle might have known what Billy had tried to do to Slocum and then proceeded to ignore it.

"You with us or you staying here?" Slocum shoved his six-gun into his holster.

"I . . ." Lyle began stammering and looking around. If pressed on the matter, he was more likely to quit than to ride at his boss's side.

"You stay and look after things here," Peter Helmann said, seeing his new foreman's lack of enthusiasm for a fight. "Gretchen, you and Lyle see to getting things back to normal here. From what I can make out, Uwe was going to sell all the cattle, then put the Circle H up for sale. Cancel all those orders."

"I'll ride with you, Papa," she said. Gretchen cast a side-long glance at Slocum, daring him to object.

Slocum was already going to fetch his horse. He had no more time for her petty concerns. He had a man to kill.

"Saddle one for me, too, Slocum," called Peter Helmann.

"Saddle your own," Slocum said. "Time's wasting."

He got his horse from the barn, and couldn't help looking down at the hay bale where Gretchen had been bent over only a few minutes earlier. The warmth in his loins had been replaced by a coldness that told him it was time to settle the score with Billy. If Uwe Helmann got in the way, too bad for him. But Slocum wanted Billy.

Slocum rode past the tight knot of cowboys. Gretchen stared at him as he left the yard. He couldn't figure out what was going on in her head, and he didn't much care at the moment. Chances were good he wouldn't be back this way any time soon. If the Texas Ranger didn't dog his tracks too much, Slocum vowed to get what was owed him from Laramie and Kinsley.

And he had an old man to get free of the Breiland Institute for the Insane. He had promised Evans.

"Slocum, Slocum!" called Helmann, riding hard behind him. "Wait up!"

"What do you intend to do?" Slocum asked when Peter Helmann trotted even with him.

"I want my son. You let him be."

"There's no trouble, then," Slocum said. "I want Billy. He tried to kill me in my sleep. No man gets by with that."

"You're a good man, Slocum. Thank you for what you've already done."

Slocum didn't want to listen to maudlin sentiment since it served no purpose.

"One of them rode straight ahead," Slocum said, studying the way the knee-high grass had been crushed. "Another hightailed it for those woods."

"Uwe went to the forest," Peter Helmann said in a monotone. "That was his favorite place when he was a boy. He thinks he is safe there."

"Then Billy is heading toward Austin," Slocum said, getting a fix on directions from the stars overhead. Slocum wheeled his horse in the direction Billy had taken and trotted off without another word to Peter Helmann. Let the man face his own son. Helmann had failed to confront Uwe back at the ranch. Slocum wasn't sure he wanted to see the result when Helmann succeeded because one of them would end up dead.

The clouds moved over the stars, but Slocum managed to keep after Billy. The Circle H ramrod made no effort to disguise his trail through the tall grass, but when a road cut through the fields, Slocum had to decide which direction Billy had taken. The clouds began leaking rain that came first as a light mist and then a drizzle. Slocum fumbled with his gear and pulled out his slicker. The rain bounced off the canvas and ran in small rivers down his sides, but worse was the way the rain washed away the dried blood on his forehead and opened the wound again. Slocum had to constantly swipe away new blood to keep it from getting into his eyes.

He might have been partially blind from the bullet crease, but that didn't keep him from following Billy's tracks. The ramrod had ridden along the road, but the growing mud would have hidden where he went—if Slocum hadn't already figured out what the man would do.

Slocum spotted a small grove of post oak trees and rode directly for it. There was no lightning in the clouds, but Slocum didn't think that would have deterred Billy from taking shelter here. The ramrod didn't know he had anyone on his tail, and would prefer comfort over the safety of continuing to ride as far as possible before resting.

A wry smile came to Slocum's lips when he saw the horse tethered under a tree with low-hanging limbs. Its rider couldn't be far away.

Slocum dismounted and pulled his slicker back so he could draw when it became necessary. Sneaking up on Billy and shooting him in the back wasn't something that Slocum would ever do. He wanted to look in the man's eyes when he killed him.

"Hello, Billy," he said. His words mingled with the gentle patter of raindrops against the leaves. It took the ramrod a second to realize he was no longer alone.

When he did, he shot to his feet, lost his balance in the mud, and sat heavily. Fear etched his features as he stared at Slocum.

"How'd you—?"

"You should never have tried to kill me while I was sleeping," Slocum said. "On your feet."

"Wait, Slocum, you got this wrong. It wasn't me. Uwe told me to do it. He's the one."

"On your feet or I shoot you where you're sitting," Slocum said.

"You not got the stomach to shoot a man, Slocum? Is that it? I told you it was Uwe's fault. He's the one you want. If you can kill even a snake like him."

Billy got to his feet and suddenly turned, facing away from Slocum.

"You don't have the stones to shoot a man in the back, do you, Slocum?"

Slocum waited. When Billy spun back around, Slocum went for his Colt, drew, and fired in a smooth motion. The bullet caught Billy squarely in the center of his chest. He tried to reach for the spot where Slocum's lead had ripped through him, but the six-shooter in his hand discharged. He got a shot off, but it didn't matter. Billy was already dying from Slocum's bullet.

Billy sat down again, then fell backward into the mud. Slocum walked over, kicked the six-gun from the man's hand, and then took a deep breath.

"Good riddance," Slocum said.

He returned to where he had left his horse, intending to mount and head to the Breiland Institute. He had both Kinsley and Laramie to deal with. But Slocum hesitated. With a deep sigh of resignation, he knew what he had to do before finding his one-time partners in the bank robbery.

Slocum backtracked to where he had parted company with Peter Helmann, then headed into the woods where Uwe Helmann had taken refuge. Backing up Peter Helmann wasn't something he ought to do, but Slocum felt some obligation to him for all that Helmann had endured at Poston's hands.

The rain began a thin mist again, turning the forested area into a wet, dark hell. Slocum stopped occasionally to listen for sounds ahead since he could see barely a dozen feet. When his horse began to get jittery, he knew he was getting close to somebody. Who it might be, he had no idea. Nor did Slocum know if he would shoot it out with Uwe. From everything he knew about the man, he deserved a bullet in the gut so he would die a lingering death, but he had done nothing to Slocum.

Then Slocum thought of Gretchen and her father. Uwe was worse than Billy.

He drew rein and took the time to reload his six-shooter. From ahead came small noises that were out of place, as if a man tried to move quietly through the tangled undergrowth.

Slocum dismounted and left his horse where it was since the thorny bushes were making the going increasingly painful for the horse. Slocum's tough jeans caught on the thorns and rips appeared, but he kept moving in spite of the small scratches he added to his already battered hide.

Unexpectedly, he popped into a small clearing. Slocum brought up his six-shooter and aimed it. Then he paused. The darkness masked everything. The oppressive smell of wet leaves was rivaled by a musky odor that put Slocum on edge. He didn't move any more, but planted his feet and slowly swiveled back and forth at the hips as he hunted for what had to be rampaging through the forest.

Javelina!

The tusked monster stirred in the brush ahead. Slocum cursed his stupidity in not bringing his Winchester. A six-shooter would hardly bring down one of the two-hundred-pound hogs in full charge. Long, brutal tusks could rip apart a man in a flash. Slocum gripped the butt of his six-gun and hoped that the pig wouldn't scent him.

Slocum was so keyed up that he jumped when the brush to his right suddenly parted. He aimed low, but did not squeeze off a shot. Coming from the brush was a man.

"Helmann?" Slocum called.

"Yes, here! Save me!" The Helmann answering was not Peter Helmann.

"No one will save you, Uwe," said Peter Helmann, pushing through the brush behind his son. They both stood at the far side of the small clearing, Uwe with his back to Slocum, Peter Helmann facing both him and Slocum. But the older man's attention was not on Slocum. It was on Uwe—and he had his son in the sights of his rifle.

"You sure you want to do this, Helmann?" Slocum called.

"That you, Slocum? Stay out of this. What are you doing here, anyway?"

The man's English had become so heavily accented as emotion took him that Slocum barely understood.

Uwe rattled off a staccato burst of German, but his father was unmoved. Slocum edged around to get out of the line of sight if Peter Helmann fired. Slocum doubted the man would miss at such short range, but the bullet might go through Uwe and become unpredictable.

"There's a pig out here, Helmann," Slocum warned. "Javelina."

"Please, Papa, not this. I didn't mean to do you harm. I thought it was best. You acted so . . ."

"*Verrückter?* You thought I was a crazy man? You wanted nothing but money. You would sell the Circle H, the ranch I worked to build. You would steal it!"

"Papa, no!"

Slocum sucked in his breath and held it. Peter Helmann lifted the rifle, then lowered it.

"I will let the pig eat you," Peter Helmann said.

"What?" Uwe Helmann did exactly the wrong thing. He whirled to his right and saw the red-eyed pig pushing its snout through the brush. He bolted. This drew the javelina's attention. The pig snorted, pawed the ground like a bull, then lowered its tusked head and charged.

Uwe was fast. The pig was faster. It crossed the clearing in the wink of an eye and tossed its head, raking fierce tusks across Uwe's legs. The man screeched and fell facedown on the wet ground.

Slocum heard the squish as Uwe hit the ground, and thought it might be the man's flesh ripping away. Then he realized it was only the sound of a body hitting a pile of rain-soaked leaves. Then any chance to hear such subtle noises was stolen away by Uwe's frantic cries as the javelina gored him.

The rifle shot that echoed through the forest startled Slocum. He tried to settle down, but knew he would be hard-pressed to do so with so much porcine death only a few yards away. There was no way his .36-caliber pistol would stop such a large hog.

But Peter Helmann's shot was deadly. The javelina rose

up on its hind legs, then crashed down. A second shot to its belly finished the job the first bullet had begun.

Slocum walked slowly to see what had happened to Uwe Helmann. The man's legs had been savaged. Worse, one tusk had caught him in the gut. Uwe tried to hold his intestines in. He turned a white face up to Slocum, beseeching him. He saw no mercy there. Uwe turned to his father, who was still holding the smoking rifle that had saved him from the javelina.

"Papa, thank you. You saved me."

Peter Helmann lifted the rifle and aimed it at his son.

"I did not want a pig robbing me of what I must do."

Slocum looked at the man, but saw no determination to kill his only son.

"No, Papa, you can't. Please, I beg you! I'm sorry for what I did. It was terrible." Uwe slipped into German, and then his words became incoherent as he babbled and finally cried piteously.

Peter Helmann lowered his rifle.

"It would be too kind to kill you. Leave, Uwe. Leave my land and never return. If I see you, I will finish what the pig began. I will not be so gentle."

"Papa, my legs. My belly. I can't—"

"You have been warned. Lie here and die or leave. I don't care." Peter Helmann pulled himself up and squared his shoulders. "Mr. Slocum, would you ride with me back to the ranch? I have a bottle of schnapps."

"My honor," Slocum said. He saw that Uwe Helmann might not live much longer, but Peter Helmann had washed his hands of his son. Slocum couldn't much blame him.

All the way back to the ranch house Peter Helmann never said a word. Neither did Slocum.

18

"What happened?" Gretchen Helmann stood on the porch of the ranch house with her hand at her throat. "Papa, what happened to Uwe?"

"He won't be back," Peter Helmann said. With that he pushed past his daughter and went into the house.

"John, tell me. Please." She saw he wasn't any more inclined to talk about her brother than her father had been. She took a deep breath, let it out, and then said, "I didn't expect to see you again."

"I thought I'd help out your pa, but he didn't need me," he said. Slocum sat on the porch step. Gretchen dropped down beside him so that her thigh brushed his but did not press intimately. It was as if they both needed to maintain distance.

"He's not dead," Gretchen finally said after a long pause. "I'd feel it. I would see it in Papa's face."

"Believe what your pa said. Uwe won't be back. Neither will Billy."

"You killed him. I hear that in your voice."

"He was your paramour?" Slocum asked.

"It was a while back," Gretchen said. "He turned out to be a horrible man. I don't know that he wasn't the one who came up with the plot to have Papa committed in that terrible Bedlam and then steal the ranch."

"That was Uwe's doing," Slocum said. "Billy wasn't smart enough to come up with anything like that." He started to get to his feet, but Gretchen laid her hand on his arm and stopped him.

"You don't have to go, John," she said. "I want you to stay. I . . . I can talk Papa into making you foreman. Lyle doesn't know what he's doing and will only ruin things even more."

"He'll learn. He might need some pushing and prodding to get some backbone, but he's smart enough to learn."

"I want you."

"That's something different from being foreman, isn't it?" He stared into her bright blue eyes. In the night they caught the slightest amount of light coming from inside the house and glowed with a feverish inner candescence. They both knew this wouldn't last long, but Gretchen was willing to ignore that. For the time being. Slocum couldn't because he had some bloody chores that needed to be done.

"Hey, Slocum, you back so soon?" Lyle came up. "I jist heard from an outrider that there's a whole slew of Texas Rangers out there, not five miles off."

"You mean Texas Ranger," Gretchen said. "Ranger Coldcreek is back?"

"Nope, there's a company of them. Ten, maybe more."

Slocum was surprised. Texas Rangers bragged on how few it took to uphold the law and to track down outlaws. "One riot, one Ranger," was the way he had always heard it.

"Wilson must have lit a real fire under them," Slocum said. He considered Gretchen's offer. Staying now as foreman was entirely out of the question. The first time one of the Rangers came by, lead would fly.

"Don't know nuthin' 'bout any of that, Slocum, but you sorta gave me the feelin' they was huntin' fer you."

"I have business," Slocum said, "but can you do me a favor?"

"Tell 'em you went the other way?" suggested Lyle.

"Just the opposite," Slocum said. "If they ask after me or men named Laramie, Kinsley, or Carbuncle, you tell them all about the Breiland Institute and how Mr. Helmann was kept there illegally."

"But it was legal! The sheriff and the judge were in cahoots with Uwe," protested Gretchen.

"Tell them everything—and that I am there hiding out."

"You want the Rangers to come after you? Why?" Gretchen looked aghast.

"Because I won't be there, but Poston, Ludmilla, and all the rest of them filthy kidnappers will be."

"Mr. Evans," Gretchen said weakly. "He's still there. I forgot him. So there might be others like him and Papa who've been locked up for no reason other than to get them out of the way."

"The Rangers won't cotton much to what the sheriff—or Poston—has done. Setting them on my trail will be good enough to start them poking around the Institute," Slocum said. He thrust out his hand for Lyle to shake. "I appreciate the warning."

"I don't git it, Slocum, but if you want me to tell them Rangers what you jist said, I will."

"Only if they ask," Slocum said. Lyle went off, scratching his head as he tried to understand what was going on.

"Be safe, John," Gretchen said. She gave him a quick peck on the cheek, then raced into the house. Slocum stared after her, wondering if he'd made a mistake. He came to a swift conclusion. Leaving her on the Circle H was not wrong when he had owlhoots like Laramie and Kinsley to settle accounts with.

Slocum didn't bother asking when he took a spare horse. The time would come real soon when he had to ride far and fast. He needed a fresh horse to ride while his rested from carrying him and his gear.

Riding into the sable night, Slocum was glad that the

rain had let up. The heavy clouds threatened more, but he ignored this as he made a beeline for the Institute. He wanted to reach it before sunrise, if he could.

Lightning lit the predawn sky and thunder crashed like heavy wagons rumbling across the Hill Country. The bolts that raced from one side of the sky to the other lit the Breiland Institute strangely, as if ghosts flittered about. Slocum wasn't superstitious, but he had to shiver at the sight. He tried to pass it off as rain dribbling down his neck, but knew going back into that viper's pit was the last thing he wanted to do.

But he had no choice.

Riding slowly along the walls surrounding the Institute, he found the spot where he had entered before. The heavy rain had caused the toe- and handholds to crumble. Scaling the wall here would be even more of a trial than before. He rode on, then suddenly reversed course. Take the bull by the horns. That was the only way of reaching an end to this.

Slocum rode through the front gate, hunting for guards. The rain had driven them all inside. Even the one usually stationed in the turret was missing. As Slocum reached for his rifle, he froze.

"Wondered if you might git yer ass on back here," Kinsley said. "I bet Laramie fifty dollars you would. He said you was too cowardly, that you was prob'ly already across the Rio Grande and knocking back tequila, tryin' to drown yer sorrow at havin' lost so much money."

"Funny," Slocum said. "Carbuncle said about the same thing—before I ran my knife into his belly."

Kinsley reacted as Slocum had expected. There was a flash of shock, then the man went for his six-shooter. The hesitation was all Slocum needed to roll out of the saddle and put his horse between them.

"Git on out where I kin shoot you," Kinsley said.

Slocum saw the man's boots approaching. Slocum drew his six-shooter and fired into Kinsley's left foot. The outlaw let out a yelp of pain that gave Slocum plenty of time to duck down under his horse's belly and unload a punch with his left hand that ended on Kinsley's chin. The outlaw rocked back, tried to keep his balance, and had his gunshot foot give way under him. He hit the ground hard.

Slocum aimed his six-gun directly at him.

"Move and you're a dead man."

"You don't have the guts to shoot an unarmed man." Kinsley looked to the mud where his six-gun had fallen.

"That's what Billy said. He was wrong, too."

"Billy? Who the hell's Billy?"

"Another fool who tried to ambush me," Slocum said.

"It wasn't my idea. Laramie did it—" Kinsley flopped onto his side and made a grab for his pistol. Slocum shot him before his fingers touched the cold metal. Kinsley slumped, facedown in the mud. He blew a bubble or two and then finally died.

Slocum rolled him over and searched his pockets. He found forty dollars in greenbacks and some small silver coins. This was a start on getting back his share of the loot from the bank robbery.

Slocum stared at the dead outlaw and wondered if he would ever even the score with the banker in Austin. Making sure Wilson never saw any of the money Laramie had stolen would go a ways toward paying him back, but Slocum knew their paths would have to cross eventually. He was a man who carried a grudge for a long, long time.

He was also a man who always kept his promise. Stepping over Kinsley, he went to the huge double doors leading into the Institute and pushed against them hard. They swung open, letting him slip into the lobby. Slocum had spent far too much time within these walls. He wished he could burn the whole damned place to the ground, but it wouldn't happen tonight.

Slocum started to go around the stairs leading to the second floor to get into the wing where Evans was being held, but he saw that the door to Poston's office stood ajar. He licked his lips, then turned to the office. A grin spread as he thought of rifling through the desk and finding where Dr. Poston kept the money needed to run the Institute.

Going into the office was like another cold wind blowing across his senses. He had searched this office before and not found anything, but he'd had more than enough time to think about where Poston would hide a safe. The man had trapdoors into escape tunnels—death tunnels—below the Institute. There must be a fake panel in the office. It fit with the way Poston thought.

Slocum closed the office door and looked around. The wall shared by the lobby was not a good choice, nor were the side walls with rooms on either side. That left the wall behind the director's desk. Tapping with the butt of his pistol quickly revealed a hollow spot. Slocum ran his fingers around the paneling, but jerked back when he cut his finger.

"There," he said to himself. He had sliced open his finger on the panel release. He pressed into it again, this time avoiding the sharp edge. A tiny *pop!* sounded as the fake wall snapped open. Slocum swung the small door wide and glared at the safe inside the hidden nook. The vault in Wilson's bank had hardly been stronger. The difference was obvious, though. Wilson's vault had been open. All Laramie, his partners, and Slocum had needed to do was waltz in, collect the money, and then get the hell out.

Poston's vault was securely fastened. Tapping the butt of his pistol against combination dial told Slocum it would take a couple sticks of dynamite to blow this open. He didn't have any explosive. He needed the combination. The only one likely to know it was the director himself.

Closing the fake wall panel, Slocum knew he had to finish off other chores before worrying about this. Laramie still walked free. But Slocum wanted to find Evans and free the old man. He crossed the lobby and went around the stairs to the door leading into the wing where he had found Peter Helmann. Six-shooter ready, he opened the door. The two guards he had seen before were once more at the table. His sudden entry woke them.

"Don't move," Slocum said. "I don't want to waste lead on you."

"D-don't shoot, mister. Who are you?" The guard who was more awake than his partner put his hands in the air.

"Your worst nightmare if you try anything. Open the door to the cell block."

"We don't have the keys," said the other one.

Slocum stepped up and swung his six-gun, striking the man on the cheek.

"Ouch," the man said, grabbing his face. He looked up and saw Slocum's face glaring at him like a bloody mask. Slocum had been through hell and had come out the other side in the past twenty-four hours. His appearance was enough to put the fear in anyone.

"I got 'em here, right here, mister. Really," said the other guard. He picked up a key ring and held it out. His hand shook.

"You've got five seconds to get the door open."

The guard took ten because of his nerves, but Slocum wasn't that much of a stickler. The guard was doing what he wanted, doing it as fast as he could. That suited Slocum. He herded the two of them down the corridor to Evans's cell.

"Get him out."

"Evans? But—"

Slocum slugged the guard. The other obeyed, pulling open the door.

"Come on out, Mr. Evans," Slocum called. The old man edged out, his rheumy eyes darting about. When he finally spotted Slocum, he smiled broadly.

"Damn me, you came back."

"Stow these two inside, lock them up, then you hightail it and find Ranger Coldcreek."

"Coldcreek? The half-Injun Ranger?"

"Never heard that," Slocum said. "Doesn't matter a whit to me. He'll be interested in what's been going on here if you tell him the men who robbed the bank in Austin are hiding out here."

"I'll tell that varmint more 'n that!"

"Just do it," Slocum said. He made sure the old man had the guards secured in the cell, then headed back for the lobby. Finding Laramie was more important than ever, if Evans found his way outside and brought the law here. Slocum wanted to be done with his business and on the trail to Mexico before the Texas Rangers showed up to clean out this hellhole.

"Hey, you, thank you kindly!" called Evans. The old man waved a wrinkled hand. Slocum touched the brim of his hat, then slipped out of the guardroom back to the lobby. He had no idea how much havoc Evans would cause if he was spotted on his way off the grounds, but the guards would come swarming out of their holes like ants.

Slocum stopped at the base of the stairs when he heard the soft scurry-scurry of feet moving upward. He craned his neck and tried to catch sight of whoever had just gone up the stairs, but they were moving too fast. He wasn't ready to begin a shoot-out quite yet. He had done his duty getting Evans out of his cell, but the lure of the safe in Poston's office called to him.

Laramie might have stashed the money from the robbery there. He had certainly handed over a significant chunk of it to Poston for the privilege of hiding out in the asylum while the law hunted all over the Texas Hill Country for him.

Slocum went back to the office, then stopped and stared. Anger rising, he began cursing as he went to the hidden panel. It stood open a few inches. Slocum was sure he had secured it before going after Evans. He pushed it open, and his stomach flopped over. The safe door was also open.

He didn't have to look to know the safe had been emptied. But he checked.

"Empty," he said in disgust.

He heard the telltale click of a six-shooter cocking behind him. Slocum had been decoyed into an ambush.

19

"I've wanted to do this for quite a while," Dr. Poston said.

Slocum considered his chances. They didn't appear too good.

"Why'd you take everything out of the safe?" Slocum asked.

"What? You stole my money," Poston said, moving around. "Keep your hands high, Slocum. I don't mind shooting you in the back." Poston came to a spot where he could look past Slocum into the empty safe. "What'd you do with it? Where's the money? *My* money!"

"It was empty. I came in about ten minutes ago and the safe was locked. When I got back, it was open and like this." Slocum moved to tap the empty shelf inside.

"You're lying. You hid the money. Where is it?"

From Poston's frantic question, Slocum doubted the man was responsible for setting up a trap as he had first imagined. Pieces came together to form a bigger picture in Slocum's mind.

"I didn't steal your money. You didn't take it. Who else has the combination to the safe?" Slocum asked.

"Nobody. Only I—" Poston cut off his words.

"Ludmilla," guessed Slocum. "She figured out the combination, didn't she?"

"She must have seen the combination the last time I dialed it. I was in a hurry and never thought she would do this to me. We are partners. Were partners," he said with a rising anger.

"She's really taken a shine to Laramie, hasn't she? Some women might find a man like that mighty attractive." Slocum was shooting in the dark, but he hit a bull's-eye with his guess about what was going on upstairs. Poston roared in anger.

"We've got a mutual enemy, Poston," Slocum hurried on. "I want him for double-crossing me."

"He's mine. She's mine," Poston said in an ugly tone.

"We can do it together. All I want is my cut from the robbery."

"You were in on the robbery Laramie and his partners pulled in Austin?"

"They tried to set me up to be the one caught by the Texas Ranger," Slocum said. "I thought something was fishy since they didn't need a fourth to pull off such an easy bank robbery, but they knew Ranger Coldcreek was in the area and he would never rest until he caught them."

"They used you as a cat's-paw," Poston said. "It's something Ludmilla would think of."

"It was all Laramie's doing," Slocum said. Then he saw a chance to drive a wedge even harder between Poston and the madam. "Unless Laramie has been here before, maybe as one of Ludmilla's customers. How did he happen to hear that you would hide him from the law?"

"There's a steady flow of them through the Institute," Poston said. His six-shooter drifted from dead center on Slocum's back as he talked. "I use Ludmilla to recruit. She hears things and passes along invitations. She could have seen Laramie before, but I'm not certain."

"They're in cahoots," Slocum said.

"Dammit!" cried Poston. "She's done this to steal all my hard-earned money!"

Slocum kept silent on how the money had been "earned." He was in no position to pass judgment on how he had come by the money in contention with Laramie, either.

"Looks like we're in the same wagon heading the same direction," Slocum said. "Laramie and Ludmilla are robbing us both."

"No!" shrieked Poston. "I won't allow it!"

"Where would they be right now? I heard somebody with a light tread going up the stairs before I came in here. That might have been Ludmilla, or one of her whores."

"It's her. It's got to be. No one else could have stolen the combination." Dr. Poston came closer. Slocum tensed, thinking he could jump the man and wrest the gun from his hands. But all Poston wanted was a closer look at the safe to be certain Slocum had not somehow forced it open and then taken the money. Slocum let him get a gander at the empty shelf and the way the door swung open easily, the locking bolts all withdrawn into the sides of the safe door.

"You want some help?" Slocum asked.

"I can kill them on my own." Poston lifted the pistol, ready to cut Slocum down.

"They made a fool out of you mighty easy," Slocum said. "Me, too. I want to even the score and can back you up."

"Why should I trust you?"

"I hate Laramie more than I do you. I'd never set eyes on you until that first day when I blundered in here. You thought I was looking for Ludmilla's brothel, but I didn't have any idea what was going on. All I wanted to do was track Laramie and his gang."

"They led you straight to the Institute," Poston said, his anger growing visibly. "The fools! I warned them about entering from different directions."

"Right up to your front door," Slocum said. He saw how Poston's aim wavered now. Any intention the doctor had of shooting Slocum vanished with the need to get his revenge on Ludmilla and Laramie.

"The other one, Kinsley. We need to worry about him.

He's a stone killer. I knew that from the instant he and Laramie walked in."

"I'll guard your back. You don't need to worry about Kinsley," Slocum said, more truth in his words than he wanted to reveal to Poston. "You find Laramie. And Ludmilla."

"Come on." Poston motioned with his six-gun, keeping Slocum in front of him. It wasn't the best position to be when a trigger-happy madman was so close behind, but Poston hadn't taken away the Colt Navy or the knife in his boot. That suited Slocum just fine. For the moment. He'd even let Poston shove him into the viper's den and shoot it out with Laramie. Only after the outlaw and Ludmilla were taken care of was there reason to worry.

Slocum took the steps to the second-floor landing two at a time. He paused when he reached the second story, listening hard for any sounds that might signal an attack. He heard people moving about, but nothing threatening.

"The girls all have rooms on this floor," said Poston. "When they're not upstairs, they are here."

"Why not have the brothel here and the Cyprians' rooms on the third?" Slocum asked. To him that made more sense than having the brothel's patrons climb an extra floor, passing the rooms used only for sleeping.

"Control," Doctor Poston said. "Running the Institute is all about control. If any trouble happens, we can shut off the staircase and keep it contained upstairs. Nobody will escape to tell the law about this place."

"Must cost an arm and a leg," said Slocum, "paying off the sheriff and the judge the way you do." For an instant he thought he had pushed Poston too far. The doctor stopped and held his six-shooter out at arm's length, as if he were a duelist ready to fire at his opponent.

"Sometimes the overhead isn't too onerous," Poston said. "An hour every now and then with a favorite girl is all the judge requires."

"So he'll commit anybody you ask in return for a tumble in the hay?"

Poston laughed nastily. "The sheriff is hardly better. He has no idea that we put up outlaws like this was some sort of fancy hotel. He thinks the whorehouse is the only illegal activity here. I pay him to look the other way, and he doesn't suspect a thing."

"You've got the whole county sewn up tight," Slocum said. He didn't bother keeping the admiration from his voice. Poston had raked in the money from all takers for some time. Slocum wasn't sorry to see it all come tumbling down around the man's head, not when he locked up sane men like Evans and Peter Helmann for money. This was far worse, in Slocum's mind, than shooting a man in the back.

"Quiet," said Poston. "Listen. I hear them upstairs."

"Sounds like Ludmilla's packing her bags. Reckon she and Laramie are getting ready to leave. That must mean she's contacted the Texas Rangers."

"Why'd she do that?"

"To tidy up loose ends," Slocum said. "If she and Laramie have the money from the safe—and the money he stole from the bank—you're the loose end. You and me." Slocum kept coming back to how he and Poston shared the same enemies. With the man waving the six-shooter around the way he was doing, it wouldn't take much for him to start firing wildly.

"They're too cowardly to even do their own dirty work," Poston muttered as he mulled over what Slocum had said. "They would call in the law, from either Austin or San Antonio. Ludmilla knows the sheriff would never arrest me. Why kill the goose that lays the golden egg?"

Slocum slowed on the stairs leading to the third-floor sitting room where he had first met Ludmilla. Every step was cautiously planted to keep from accidentally finding a squeaky step that would alert them. From the noises coming from the sitting room, though, Slocum doubted much would interrupt Laramie and Ludmilla.

"I'll kill them!" roared Poston when he heard the amorous sounds Slocum already had. The doctor rushed up the stairs, waving his six-shooter around. When he got to the top of the stairs, he began firing.

Slocum followed warily. He saw that Laramie had taken cover behind a fainting couch. The outlaw's pants were dropped on the floor next to his boots and his six-shooter. Ludmilla was entirely naked. Slocum had to admit that she was one lovely woman, but she was also on her way to being a very dead one.

"You betrayed me, with that . . . that—" Dr. Poston sputtered so much the words wouldn't come out properly. He looked like a rabid weasel ready to go on a biting, snarling rampage.

"It's not like that, really," Ludmilla said. She held her hands in front of her, then moved them to her flaring hips. She cocked one hip forward, frankly displaying her charms. One hand remained on her hip and the other cupped a breast, bouncing it in what she hoped would be an enticing manner.

"You were with him!"

"He's a guest here," Ludmilla said. "You know that I entertain *your* guests. It's part of our bargain."

"You were conniving with him. You robbed my safe!"

Slocum saw Ludmilla turn pale.

"You weren't supposed to be back from town until sundown," she said in a small, little-girl voice.

"You were screwing him and you stole my money!"

Slocum wondered which was worse in Poston's mind. Probably that Ludmilla had betrayed him by taking the money from the safe.

"You got careless, Poston," Laramie called from behind the couch. "I tole you to watch what you were doin'."

Poston fired at the man. The bullet tore through the fabric and the padding beneath, but missed the outlaw.

"Did you notify the half-breed Ranger?" Poston shouted. "Is Coldcreek on the way here?"

Slocum hadn't thought Ludmilla could blanch any more than when Poston had accused her of robbing the safe, but she did. Trembling, whiter than a sheet, she moved to cover her breasts, her privates, to turn away as if suddenly ashamed.

"Laramie, do something! He knows!"

"Shut up, bitch!" roared the outlaw. "If he hadn't known before, he knows everything now!"

Slocum edged along the wall to get a good shot at Laramie. He didn't cotton much to killing an unarmed, naked man, but in Laramie's case he would make an exception.

Then everything changed. Fast. Ludmilla had been looking all shy and embarrassed one instant. The next she was a screaming, spitting wildcat raking her nails down Poston's face. Poston staggered back and crashed into Slocum, knocking him hard into the wall. Poston's six-shooter went off and Ludmilla gasped, and then there was the sound of bare feet running across carpeted floor and up the spiral staircase leading to Ludmilla's private assignation room.

"Stop, stop!" Poston screeched, trying to stanch the blood flowing from three parallel scratches on his cheek. He fired twice more. The bullets ricocheted around but did not come close to Ludmilla. The last Slocum saw of her was her naked rear end and legs disappearing around the final turn in the spiral staircase.

"Wait," Slocum said, grabbing for Poston. The doctor shoved him back to the floor and charged after Ludmilla. Slocum got to his feet and again tried to stop Poston. The doctor flew around the stairs.

"My money, give me my money, you bitch!" Poston shouted as he went up into the turret.

Slocum saw a carpetbag on the floor near Ludmilla's dress and grabbed it as he followed Poston.

"Here it is," Slocum said, but Poston was past hearing. Or caring.

Slocum swung around the three turns in the staircase in time to see Poston wrestling with Ludmilla. Her bare flesh shone in the light of the sun, turning it golden. She tried to force the six-gun away, but Poston was too strong. He brought it up. With a convulsive heave, she lifted the small man and slammed him into a window. The etched glass shattered all around him, cascading down like crystalline rain.

Poston looked down at his belly. Ludmilla had forced the muzzle around and the doctor had shot himself. His lips curled into a sneer as he lifted the six-shooter and pulled the trigger. The hammer fell on a dud. He cocked and fired again. Empty. With a roar, Poston launched himself, caught Ludmilla in a bear hug, and carried her backward.

Backward through another window. Locked together, they crashed through the window. Both screamed all the way to the ground three stories below. Then there was only silence.

Slocum hurried to the window and looked down. Poston had landed atop the woman. From the crazy angles of arms, legs, and necks, he knew they were both dead. He backed away, still clutching the carpetbag. Slocum opened it and smiled. He had been right about the contents. There was more money here than he had ever dreamed of.

Money from the whorehouse, from the illegal imprisonment of men like Peter Helmann, from sheltering outlaws from the law.

"Laramie!" Slocum had forgotten all about the outlaw until he had looked at the money in the carpetbag. He jumped up, sat on the iron railing, and slid down and around to the sitting room level.

Laramie had hightailed it. Literally. His pants and boots were still on the floor, but his six-shooter was missing from his holster.

Slocum started for the stairs, then slowed and finally sneaked a quick peek around the corner. He was glad he had been so cautious. Laramie crouched on the landing, waiting. The outlaw fired at Slocum.

"Don't waste too many rounds, Laramie," Slocum called. "You can't reload, unless you got bullets hidden where the sun don't shine." This brought two more shots. Slocum ventured around and got a shot at Laramie, sending the naked man scampering down to the second floor. From the sound of bare feet hitting the stair steps, he wasn't slowing down.

Slocum followed in time to get off a shot as Laramie tried to get through the huge double doors leading outside. Splinters from the shot near his head caused Laramie to duck and whirl around. He fired twice more. Then he came up empty.

"Carry an empty chamber so the hammer won't set off a round accidentally?" called Slocum. "That's real smart out on the trail. It's downright dumb now, isn't it?"

Laramie let out a screech of anger and lit out for the door leading into the wing behind the stairs, where Evans and Peter Helmann had been kept.

Slocum jumped the balustrade and landed heavily just behind Laramie. He fired. The naked outlaw got through the door just in time. The bullet ripped into metal but did no harm. Slocum considered reloading, but he didn't want Laramie finding some way out. The entire Institute was honeycombed with the subterranean passages and he had no idea how many of them Laramie had scouted. He dropped the carpetbag with the money and went after Laramie.

He ran to the door and flung it open. He fired point-blank into Jonah's face. The huge baby-faced guard staggered back, sat down in a chair, and simply stared ahead. Dead.

Slocum gave the guardroom a quick look to be sure Laramie wasn't hiding there. He opened the inner door and saw the rows of cells on either side. His nose wrinkled. He had forgotten the stench from the offal and the dead. And the raucous cries of the demented. Laramie had riled them. Now Slocum was adding to their upset.

He went down the row of doors, looking in each grille and being sure the locking bar was in place. Only one cell door was unbarred. Slocum went to it and looked into the cell through the grille. It was the one Evans had been kept in. Slocum looked around but saw nothing. He backed away, cocked his six-shooter, and waited a heartbeat for what he knew would happen. Laramie couldn't be anywhere else but hunkered down against the door, out of sight through the grille.

Laramie burst from the cell, intent on grabbing Slocum from behind. Instead he found himself staring into the muzzle of the Colt.

"You're not dressed for this shindig," Slocum said. He pointed to a straightjacket dangling on a peg. "Put it on."

"The hell you say. Git it over with, Slocum. Shoot me!"

Laramie rushed him. Slocum sidestepped and tripped the man, sending him to the floor. Swinging the barrel of his six-gun hard, he landed it right behind Laramie's ear. All the fight went out of the owlhoot.

Slocum grabbed the restraint and took his time putting it on. He cinched up the arms behind Laramie's back as tightly as he could, then added a touch of his own. He crammed a filthy rag into the man's mouth and fastened it in place with a length of rawhide strap he found on the floor. Grunting with the effort, he dragged Laramie to an adjoining empty cell and left him in a pile in the middle of the tiny room. Slocum counted his lucky stars that he had remembered how Evans had escaped his cell. Laramie wouldn't get the chance to squeeze through the hole caused by the missing block. This cell's walls were intact.

He slammed the door, barred it, and thrust in the cotter pin to keep it from opening by accident. As he looked back in, he saw Laramie's eyes wide with fear.

"Don't worry. If you're lucky, the Texas Ranger might

find you. If you're not so lucky, you might spend the rest of your goddamn life in there!" Slocum turned and walked off, ignoring the mumbled pleas from within the cell.

He passed Jonah and got to the lobby, where he picked up the carpetbag filled with money. Slocum had started for the front doors when he heard horses outside. Lots of them. Ranger Coldcreek's sharp voice carried. Slocum ducked into Poston's office, found the trapdoor, and dropped to the tunnel below.

It took the better part of an hour for him to find his way out to the barn, but he doubted the Ranger would think of looking for a tunnel when he had plenty of other things to check out in the Breiland Institute for the Insane.

Slocum climbed out of the tunnel, but saw no way out other than over the wall. He hated leaving behind his horse, as well as the second one he had taken from the Circle H remuda, but leaving now was his only hope for getting away from the Ranger. Slocum got over the wall and dropped down, only to hear a soft voice.

"Going somewhere, Slocum?"

He turned and saw Gretchen.

"You aren't getting away from me this easy, mister," she said.

"You brought the Ranger?"

"I insisted on leading him and the others here. Six Rangers. You should be honored."

"I'd feel a lot better if my horses weren't inside."

"I'll get them back," Gretchen said. She dismounted and came to him. "For a price."

He kissed her. Or did she kiss him? It didn't matter. When she backed away, her eyes were still half-closed. A deep sigh escaped her.

"Take my horse. I'll think of something to tell Coldcreek."

"Here," Slocum said, handing her the carpetbag. "Give this to Evans and anyone else who's been kept in that hellhole."

Before she could take the handle, Slocum opened it and fished out the amount of money Wilson had stolen from him. Eight hundred dollars. "This is mine. Not stolen."

"Does it matter?" she asked.

"Does to me," Slocum said. He thought about kissing her ruby lips again, then decided he might not want to leave if he did. Swinging into the saddle, he turned the pony's face west, toward the Rio Grande, toward sanctuary in Mexico beyond the Texas Rangers' jurisdiction.

Slocum touched the brim of his hat, then galloped off into the twilight. He could be in Mexico in a couple days, but it would take a lot longer for him to forget Gretchen Helmann.

Watch for

SLOCUM AND THE LAND-GRABBERS

333rd novel in the exciting SLOCUM series
from Jove

Coming in November!